The Silver Crown

The Silver Crown

ROBERT C. O'BRIEN

COLLIER BOOKS
Macmillan Publishing Company
New York

Collier Books

Macmillan Publishing Company

866 Third Avenue, New York, NY 10022

Collier Macmillan Canada, Inc.

First Aladdin Books edition 1973

First Collier Books edition 1988

Printed in the United States of America

The alternate ending of *The Silver Crown* first appeared in the British edition, first published in hardcover in 1973 by Victor Gollancz, Ltd.

10 9 8 7 6 5 4 3

Library of Congress Cataloging-in-Publication Data

O'Brien, Robert C.

The silver crown / Robert C. O'Brien—1st Collier Books ed.

p.   cm.

Summary: On her tenth birthday, Ellen wakes up to find a silver crown on her pillow; a few minutes later her house burns up, her parents disappear, and she is launched on an adventure involving a trek through the woods, a castle full of brainwashed captives, and the powerful Hieronymus Machine which wants her crown.

ISBN 0-02-044651-9

[1. Fantasy.] I. Title.

PZ7.0135Si 1988

[Fic]—dc19   88-2837

CIP

AC

For my children and, someday, their children

Contents

The Silver Crown

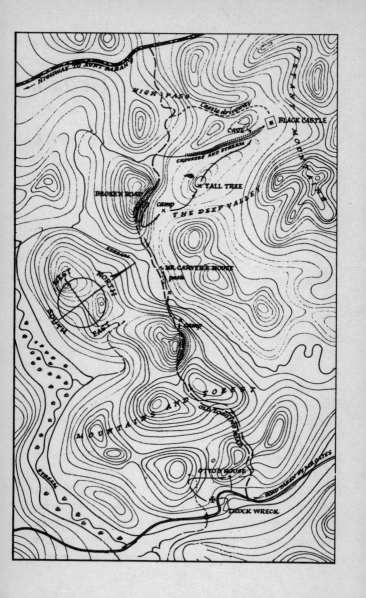

The Birthday Present

SHE had known all along that she was a queen, and now the crown proved it. It was the first thing she saw when she opened her eyes; it lay beside her on the pillow, shinier than silver, glowing softly, with twinkling blue stones set all around. And although it looked hard and solid, when she touched it she discovered that the silvery metal was actually a finely spun fabric, strong but soft as silk, so that if she wanted to, she could fold the whole crown in the palm of her hand and tuck it in her pocket.

She got out of bed, stood in front of the mirror, and put it on her head. It felt light and warm and comfortable. Of course it fitted her perfectly.

Her name was Ellen; she had brown hair, gray eyes, clean teeth, rather knobby knees, and was 55½ inches tall. She was ten years old; yesterday she had been nine, but today was her birthday, and the crown was her first present. It did not occur to her to wonder from whom it had come; she was merely aware that it was hers by right.

Her bedroom, a white room with a slanted ceiling, was in the attic floor of the house. Her parents, her brother and her younger sister all had their beds on the floor below. She looked at her clock; it was not yet quite seven and she knew, now that school was out, that they would all still be asleep. It was not *their* birthday.

She got dressed, brushed her hair for seven seconds with no noticeable effect, slipped the crown into her pocket and started downstairs. Halfway down she turned around and came back up. She took the crown from her pocket, where it made a sizable bulge (also, though it was light on her head, it felt heavy in her pocket), and put it instead into a red leather pocketbook, which she snapped shut and slipped over her wrist. Besides the crown the pocketbook held a dollar and fifty-six cents. She hoped it would hold more before the birthday ended. It also contained a tattered letter from her Aunt Sarah, who was beautiful, lived in the mountains (but who traveled a great deal), and was the only grownup who knew—honestly knew, and did not just pretend to know—that Ellen was a queen.

Ellen went down to the kitchen, where she ate a doughnut in four bites and drank half a glass of milk. She slipped another doughnut into the pocket where the crown had been and went out the front door, closing it quietly behind her.

Outside, the morning was still faintly misty and the neighborhood was asleep. She took the crown from her purse, adjusted it on her head, and started down the sidewalk at a queenly pace. Then, about a block ahead she thought she saw someone moving; she had the odd impression that whoever it was had a green head. When she looked again she could see no one, so it must have been only some leaves moving in the wind. Nonetheless, feeling rather self-conscious, she took the crown off again as she walked in the direction of the royal palace.

She came in a few minutes to a small wooded park, which she entered. Through the woods, she walked to a clearing where there lay a comfortable log, or rather a royal bench, for this was the castle garden; when she sat on the bench the castle stood behind her, just over her right shoulder, out of sight beyond the trees. She put on her crown and almost immediately a brown and white rabbit, whom she knew slightly, emerged from the woods on the far side of the clearing, made a sweeping obeisance toward the queen, and hopped away down an invisible rabbit-run on business of his own. The queen encouraged wildlife in the royal park—rabbits, squirrels, birds, butterflies, slugs, spiders (she did not really encourage the last two, but they were there anyway)—and she allowed no hunting.

Although the castle was out of sight, she knew exactly what it looked like. It had three tall towers, all minareted, and two shorter ones standing guard over the portcullis, which had a spiked iron gate ready to crash shut, and, of course, a drawbridge wide enough to accommodate mounted chargers three abreast. The curtain wall was gracefully buttressed, and in the clear blue water of the moat swam ducks, geese, swans and fish; it also contained a small boat in which the queen could, when the mood took her, go paddling. One of the towers (the one over the keep) was haunted by the ghost of the Old Duke, an evil man who had, back in the Middle Ages, put three wives to the knife before they caught and hanged him.

All in all, it looked quite a lot like a famous castle called Neuschwanstein, which stands high in the Alps, in Europe, and was built by King Ludwig II of Bavaria, later called Ludwig the Mad because he spent most of the royal treasure building castles he didn't need. Neuschwanstein was his grandest; Ellen's Aunt Sarah, while traveling in the Alps, had once sent her a postcard with a picture of it, and Ellen thought it the most beautiful place she had ever seen.

Though her castle had in its Great Hall a Chamber of State one hundred feet long, with a gold throne on a dais at one end, Ellen preferred to hold court, when the weather was fine, in the garden. She would do so today, she decided, and since the courtiers would be gathering soon, she went over in her mind the agenda for the morning.

First the Prime Minister, probably accompanied by the Colonial Secretary, would want to discuss Affairs of State, including reports from remote outposts of the empire—places like the Fiji Islands, Borneo, or the Outer Hebrides, where there sometimes were native uprisings. Then the Chancellor of the Exchequer, an interminable man, would ask her to approve a long list of figures pertaining to taxes, death rates, appropriations, the crown debt, income from royal holdings, and (reprovingly) royal expenditures. This was rather like arithmetic and always got Ellen feeling slightly dizzy.

Next the Royal Steward, with the Grand Duke and

Duchess (a dashing young couple), would discuss arrangements for the Queen's Ball, now only two weeks off and thus fearfully urgent. When the Chancellor of the Ex. was out of earshot, the Queen planned to ask the Duchess, who was not only her Chief Lady-in-Waiting but also her best friend, to find out the price of a new ermine robe she must have for the ball.

Her planning was interrupted suddenly by the wail of a fire siren, then another, then a third, and engines rumbling down the street next to the park. Ellen now had lived in the city long enough (more than three weeks) so that she no longer got excited about fire engines. She heard their sirens nearly every day, but in town, unlike the country, they merely shrieked off somewhere out of sight and put out a small fire in the house or apartment of someone you didn't know.

So she sat still and waited for the noise to fade in the distance, when she could resume planning for the ball. But this time it did not fade, at least not very far. She heard the sirens whine down from treble to bass and then stop, still within earshot. There was a lot of confused shouting, and then the loud throb of an engine—a pump? Two more sirens screamed, coming from another direction. Then she smelled smoke.

It must be *near,* she thought. She could not possibly hold court in such a ruckus, so she decided to go and look. Official business, including the ball, would have to wait until afternoon; she could only hope the park would still be empty. It was next to impossible to hold court with a lot of children playing around.

She stood up from the log, put the crown back in her

pocketbook, and walked out through the woods. Down the street, in the direction from which she had come, the fire engines—five of them—were pulled up at the curb. There were also a lot of firemen in black raincoats and red hats, a big crowd of people (and more coming all the time) and a policeman directing traffic.

Ellen walked quickly toward the crowd; as she got closer she began to run, her handbag banging against her legs. Then she stopped completely.

It was her house. It had burned to the ground. There was nothing left of it but some piles of blackened brick, some ashes in a hole that had once been the basement. And in the crowd around it, held back by a fence of ropes the firemen had rigged up, she saw no faces she knew.

"*I Need Help*"

Ellen walked around the edge of the crowd for a few minutes, looking for her father, her mother, her brother, David, who was thirteen and *should* be visible because he would be running, or her sister, Dorah, who was five and should be audible because she would be either shrieking or crying. But all the faces were strange, cold, and peculiarly somber. Where could her family have gone?

She walked up to one of the firemen. By this time the ashes had stopped smoking; they lay wetly, giving off a sour smell. The fireman, with two huge wrenches, was trying to uncouple two sections of hose as thick as his leg. His face was streaked with black. He strained at the wrenches. She touched his arm.

"Excuse me," she said. "I can't find my family. Do you know where they are?"

He looked up briefly. "Kid," he said, "I don't know

your family. How would I know where they are? Maybe they're home in bed."

"But I live *here*," Ellen said.

"Kid," said the fireman, *"nobody* lives here. Not any more. Burned down so fast they never knew what happened. They'll be lucky if they find some bones. I tell you what. You go on to your own house. I got work to do."

He turned and called to another fireman in a blasting voice: "Hey, Ed. Help me with this couple. I ain't Superman."

Ellen turned and walked away. She could not quite grasp what the fireman had said; she understood the words, and she did not disbelieve them, but somehow her brain refused to let them in. Then, by accident, she heard the same story again. There was a woman, standing near the rope, talking to another woman. She was wearing leather slippers and a raincoat that had been pulled on over a housecoat that had been pulled on over a night-gown; you could see the edges of each layer hanging below the next.

". . . never saw anything like it," she was saying. "I was putting the coffee in the pot and I looked out and the house was *standing* there. I turned the coffee on, looked out again, maybe three minutes, and it was gone. Just a lot of fire and smoke, as if it blew up, only no noise . . ." She turned her head, and Ellen lost a few words. Then she turned back ". . . just a few days ago; I never even learned their name. There were three or four kids. *Nobody* got out. Nobody could have . . ."

Ellen walked away and sat down on the curb a little

way from the crowd. She did not cry. She did not speak, or even move. She sat still for about ten minutes, and she may have been thinking, or she may not.

Then she got up and walked quietly back to the rope, keeping as far away from people as she could, as if she were afraid of being recognized. The crowd was thinning now; spectators were still arriving, but more were leaving; they talked only in murmers, like ghosts in a dream. Ellen walked along the rope all the way around the gray and black pile, looking hard at it, as if she were hoping to see some familiar object, even if it were burned or melted. But she saw only charcoal and ashes, some pieces of bent and twisted pipe, blackened bricks, some roof slates, and that was all.

She sat down on the curb again (she had no place else to sit) and this time she *did* think. People who walked past glanced at her, with her pocketbook dangling between her thin knees, but paid no attention. She watched the policeman, who, half a block away, was still diverting traffic while the firemen rolled up their hoses. Eventually she reached a decision, stood up, and walked firmly toward him.

"Excuse me," she said in a clear voice. "I need help."

The policeman looked down at her. He had a narrow face and a scrawny red neck, and his blue uniform shirt looked much too big at the collar. A large black pistol hung from his belt in a leather holster. But his expression was kindly enough (as if he had daughters of his own), and he answered cheerfully.

"Sure, little girl. What can I do for you?"

"My name is Ellen Carroll, and I live . . . I used to live in the house that burned down. And I can't find my father and mother."

The policeman's cheerful expression disappeared. He bent down until his face was level with Ellen's. "Are you kidding?" he said, or rather shouted. "The captain told me everybody in that house was . . . Well, never mind that. You got any identification? What did you say your name was?" Ellen repeated it as he pulled a notebook from his pocket. "Carroll's the right name, all right. You got any identification?"

Identification. That meant a card with your name and address on it, and sometimes your picture and finger-prints. Ellen had none. Then she remembered.

"I have a letter from my Aunt," she said. She took it from her handbag and then realized it was no good. It began only, "Dear Ellen"; she did not have the envelope, which had come addressed to her mother and had con-tained another letter. "It shows my first name," she said rather lamely, and handed it to him. He glanced at it; then he looked at her pocketbook. On its leather side, in faded gold script, was the letter "*C*".

"That's your initial," said the policeman.

"Yes," Ellen said. "*C* for Carroll."

"Girl," he said, "I don't know whether you're telling the truth or not, but you *look* as though you are, so I'm going to take you up to the precinct. But if this is some kid trick, the captain's going to be mad."

He walked over to a police car, which was parked nearby winking its red light on and off. There was another policeman sitting in it. They had a short conference, and then the first policeman, whose name was Officer Drogue, came back.

"He has to stay here with the radio"—indicating the other policeman—"so we'll walk to the precinct. All right? It's not very far." Ellen nodded, and they set off down the sidewalk side by side, the tall thin blue policeman and the short thin girl, her handbag bumping against her leg. After a while Officer Drogue patted her on the shoulder. "Don't you worry," he said. "We'll take care of you all right."

The Green Mask

ELLEN's mind kept plodding in a circle, like a horse in a ring. It kept saying, "My father is dead, my mother is dead, my sister is dead, my brother is dead," a sad rhyme in a nightmare; and yet at every fifth step, as she walked beside Officer Drogue's long legs, she would catch herself thinking, ". . . when we find them . . ." As if, when she got to the Precinct, there they would be; and yet she knew they would not. And then the chant would start over again.

She did not know what or where the Precinct was. She assumed it must be a house where the police lived, or possibly where the captain lived, or had his office.

Ellen's house was—had been—on a street where there were only houses, and trees and shrubs and lawns, of course; but after they walked a few blocks, they emerged into a section where the sidewalks were wider, the trees fewer, and there were a few shops and offices. Here, Ellen, who had been gazing sadly down at the sidewalk, heard a sudden shout; she looked up and saw that something very strange was happening in front of one of the shops.

It was an electric appliance store. Its door had burst open and a figure, wearing a silky, glistening green hood that hid his face, all but the eyes, ran out. Though she could not be certain, something about the way he looked and moved suggested that it was a young man, perhaps still in his teens. He paused at the curb, looked both ways, and walked quickly across the street, where he stopped and turned toward the door he had just come out. In his hand he carried a pistol with a long barrel. The shop door burst open again and another man came out. He was the store manager, dressed in a gray business suit, and he shouted as he came:

"Police! Police! Robbers! Robbers! Police!"

The man in the green hood raised his gun like a hunter, barrel across his left forearm, and fired once. There was a *crack,* and the store manager's face suddenly turned bright red; he fell and did not move.

The man in the green hood turned and ran, still holding his pistol, up the sidewalk away from Ellen, turned right into an alleyway, and disappeared.

By the time the robber began to run, Officer Drogue had already clapped his hand on Ellen's shoulder, said, "You wait here—don't move," and, drawing his own pistol, had run in pursuit. But he paused for a few hopeless seconds over the store manager, who was already dead, so that by the time he crossed the street the green hood had vanished up the alley. Officer Drogue followed, perhaps 150 feet behind, running like a boy, his gangling legs suddenly turned nimble.

Ellen stood where she was, feeling quite dizzy. In less than a minute there was another siren, and a police car came speeding up, followed by a motorcycle. Within three minutes the place was alive with police and detectives, shouting, hurrying in and out of cars, roaring off on motorcycles. In all the noise, Ellen thought she heard, several blocks away, some more gunshots, but she could not be sure. An ambulance arrived, picked up the poor, limp, dead store manager and took him away. A policeman had traced a chalk line on the sidewalk around where he lay; another took pictures with flashbulbs of the store, the body, the chalk line, and everything else. Detectives, with notebooks in their hands, knocked on the doors of the stores and houses near the electric appliance shop and asked questions. An hour went by. Officer Drogue did not come back.

Ellen stood and wondered what could have happened to him; she also wondered about an odd thing he had said —to himself, but still quite clearly—just before he ran after the robber. *"Another green hood,"* he had said, as if he had seen someone in a green hood before, perhaps earlier—perhaps near the fire?

The police and detectives began leaving, two by two in police cars, until finally there were only two left. Ellen thought she should speak to them, tell them what had happened and ask them about Officer Drogue. But just as she started toward them, they, too, got in a car and drove off. She thought there were probably some more police or detectives in the store, but when she reached the door a shade had been pulled down over the glass, and it was locked. It would not budge.

So she turned away. Without knowing quite where to go, she walked another half block past the store and came out on 30th Avenue. This was a wide, busy commercial street, with traffic lights at every corner, buses, trucks, stores and restaurants. She wandered down it until she came to a tiny triangle where grass was trying to grow and where the City Park Commission had placed two benches, their iron legs planted in concrete. She sat on one of these.

There was a restaurant across the avenue, a shabby place with a neon sign in the window that glowed— "Pizzas 'n' Pancakes"—at her. She realized she had had nothing to eat since very early in the morning, and it was now nearly noon. She did not feel hungry, but rather empty, and she knew she should eat. But eat what? Then she recalled the other doughnut in her pocket. She took it out and ate it slowly; it was too dry without milk, but it did away with the empty feeling.

The trouble was, she realized, that she did not know anyone. She had moved to the city too recently, and she did not make friends easily. What she needed was a Next of Kin, or a Relative, to act as Guardian. But there was no one here; there was only Aunt Sarah, and she was in Kentucky, at the Blue Hill, in the mountains—how many hundred miles away Ellen did not know. The thought of Aunt Sarah almost—but not quite—brought tears to Ellen's eyes. If only she were here, she would know what to do; she would find her a place to stay; she might even take her home to Kentucky.

Now Ellen tried to make herself think clearly; and

since she was a queen she found that she could, even on a day like this, even on a nearly empty stomach. As she thought, her spirit lifted a little and her dizziness, now rather like a buzzing in her head, grew less.

If Aunt Sarah was not here, it was because she did not know what had happened. Therefore the thing to do was to let her know, and the way to do that was to write her a letter.

A letter, however, would take several days to reach her, since the Blue Hill was so far out in the country. And although Ellen was sure she would come immediately, the question remained: where was Ellen herself to stay during the several days? She did not even know where to tell Aunt Sarah to look for her.

On the other hand, she did know where her aunt lived. Once, more than a year before, she had gone with her family in the car to visit the Blue Hill. Her father drove, and Ellen, in return for being allowed to sit in the front seat, had helped her mother plot the trip on the road map, and watch for signs that said Route 15, Route 77, Route 60, and finally, near the end, LEXINGTON 23 MI. They had driven through beautiful mountains and very few cities. The trip had taken two days. That time, of course, they had started from their house in the country; even so, Ellen was reasonably sure she could figure out the route again if only she had a map.

After considering the problem, she finally made a decision: she would go to Kentucky—walking when she must, but trying to get people in passing cars to give her rides. She knew about hitchhiking. When they lived in the country, her brother David had had a friend, a boy named

Michael, aged 14, whom people called wild, and maybe they were right. Anyway, one summer day Michael, with nothing to do, had gone out on the State Road and, by merely waving his thumb, had got a ride all the way to Purcellville. When he got to Purcellville he had crossed the road and, by waving his thumb in the opposite direction, got a ride back—a total distance of 140 miles, or so Michael had said. He had not told his parents about this; they thought he had gone fishing; but he had told David and Ellen. He knew a soldier, he said, who had hitchhiked all the way from California.

So Ellen now worked out a plan.

1. Write a letter to Aunt Sarah telling her not to come here, but that she, Ellen, was coming to the Blue Hill and would be there soon.

2. Get a road map. She knew that most gas stations gave them away free.

3. Buy some food. This was a problem, since she had only $1.56 in her purse; but she knew she could buy a loaf of bread for 22¢ (she had done this for her mother); and a whole loaf, she thought, ought to last three or four days—maybe even a week.

About this time her thinking was interrupted by the arrival of a tremendously fat man, who sat on the other bench, coming down so heavily on it that its iron legs creaked at the joints. He carried a large brown paper bag, which he plopped down on the seat beside him and opened, removing from it a very large pile of sandwiches and a quart bottle of orange soda pop. He stacked the sandwiches in a careful tower on a clean paper napkin, picked up the top sandwich, ate it, and reached for the second when he noticed Ellen watching him.

"Want a sandwich?" he asked, holding one out to her. "Go ahead. I got too many."

"No, thank you," said Ellen politely, but she did want one.

"Oh, have one. Peanut butter and jam. They're good." He reached over and put it on the bench beside her. Ellen picked it up.

"Thank you very much," she said. "I was a little bit hungry." And she began to eat it. She was *very* hungry. Yet while she ate half of hers, he ate three of his, each in one huge bite.

"Reason I got so many sandwiches," the fat man said, "my wife is trying to make me gain weight, I'm not fat enough already." He certainly was the fattest man Ellen had ever seen. His stomach was so big she wondered where he ever found a belt long enough to go around it; perhaps he bought two or three belts and fastened them together. His ankles oozed down over the sides of his shoes.

"You think *I'm* fat," said the man cheerfully, "you should see my wife. She's got fifty-sixty pounds on me. So she talks to me about being too fat, I just look at her and I start laughing. That shuts her up. Makes her mad. That's why she gives me so much to eat; she wants me to get fatter than she is, so she can yell at me."

He ate another sandwich and took a pull of orange soda. Then he said:

"You hear about the shooting? Right up the street. A hood in a green mask goes into a store, holds up the manager, shoots him dead. Never even stole anything, didn't even try, just looking for trouble. A cop chased him; he shot the cop too. Got clear away. This town's not safe any more. They'd even shoot a kid like you."

Ellen asked, "The cop . . . the policeman. Did he die, too?"

"Dead with one shot, right through the head. Same with the store manager. That's good shooting, for a pistol. It scares me, I'm too easy to hit." The fat man chuckled (to show he was not really scared), folded the one remaining sandwich in the paper napkin and pushed it toward Ellen. "Here. You help me lose weight." He put the empty pop bottle into the empty bag and walked away, rolling from side to side and vibrating furiously.

Ellen put the sandwich in her pocket.

Letter to Aunt Sarah

T HE clerk in the Post Office stamp window said, "No, Miss, no writing paper, only stamped envelopes and postcards." Ellen reached into her handbag and took out her small change, which consisted of one quarter, two dimes, two nickels and one penny. She also had a one-dollar bill. She gave the clerk a nickel, and got in return a plain, yellowish, stamped postcard. On the other side of the post office lobby there was a writing table with a ball point pen held to it by a chain, but no place to sit; so Ellen wrote standing up. She wrote the address first:

> Miss Sarah Carroll
> The Blue Hill
> Oakstables
> Lexington, Kentucky.

On the other side, which did not allow her very much space, she wrote:

22

"Dear Aunt Sarah:

*"Our house burned down and I have no place to stay, so
I am coming to the Blue Hill to see you and see where you
think I ought to stay. I am hitchhiking and do not know
how many days it will take as I may have to walk, so do not
worry if I do not arrive very soon."*

As she finished the note, Ellen, to her surprise, suddenly discovered that she was crying. She did not know
why, except perhaps that writing down what had happened brought it all back again. She could not feel the
tears coming, but several of them popped from her eyes
and splashed, unfortunately, on the postcard. They
smudged the ink, and when she wiped them off with her
hand, this made the smudges even blurrier, so that she
could no longer read most of the writing at all. There was
nothing to do but buy another card.

When she went back to buy it her eyes must have been
still wet, for the clerk looked at her quite sharply, and
then said with some concern:

"Is something wrong, Miss?"

The question almost made her start crying again, but
she managed to pretend to smile instead, and she said:

"No. Thank you. I just need another card." And she
gave him another nickel; this reduced her money to
$1.46, and she still had to buy the loaf of bread.

She wrote the same message over again, holding her
head this time to one side, so that the drops, if any,
would miss it. There were none, however. She signed it,
"Love, Ellen," and started to mail it. Then, for some reason she did not quite understand, she took it back and

added a postscript, in tiny handwriting because there was hardly any room left: *"P.S. I have received a silver crown for my birthday."*

She dropped the card through the slot marked, "OUT OF TOWN."

The Shiny Blue Car

D OWN 30th Avenue a few doors Ellen found a small grocery store where she bought a loaf of bread; it cost 25¢ instead of 22¢, because this was not a supermarket. That left her with only $1.21—but still she had, after all, had two free sandwiches.

Across the street from the grocery store she saw a gas station with a rack in front, and in the rack were rows on rows of road maps. She waited for the traffic light to change, and then, with her bread in a brown paper bag under her arm, she walked across.

Parked near the map-rack stood a large, new, shiny, dark blue car, behind the wheel of which sat a young man with a pleasant smile on his face.

Ellen walked up to the rack and stood before the array of maps, looking at their titles. She remembered that on their trip to Aunt Sarah's they had used several maps, and she also remembered what they were: Virginia, West

Virginia and Kentucky. She spotted Virginia and West Virginia immediately, both conveniently on the same map. She took one of these. Now to find Kentucky.

"You looked puzzled," a voice said. "I don't suppose I can help?"

It was the smiling young man, emerged from his shiny car and standing behind her. His voice was as happy as his face, though a rather high voice, young-sounding.

"Thank you," Ellen answered. "I'm trying to find a map of Kentucky, but I can't see any."

"No," said the young man, scanning the rack quickly. "There aren't any. That's because it's too far away. Most gas stations only have maps of the states near them."

He looked at the rack again and pulled out a map. "This might help." He opened it up. Its title was "South-eastern United States—Interstate Highway System."

"This has Kentucky on it, but it's not very big. It depends on what you need it for. Are you doing a geography lesson?"

"No," Ellen said. "I need it because I'm going there."

"*Are* you?" said the young man, his voice happier than ever. "Now that's strange. I'm from Kentucky myself. In fact, I'm on my way there now. I don't suppose you'd like a ride?"

He said this last very casually, as if it were really intended as a joke. But Ellen did not take it as a joke. It was, instead, an amazing piece of good luck.

"Oh," she said, almost ready to cry again, "*could* I? I was going to try to hitchhike."

The young man seemed not at all surprised to find a girl of ten planning to hitchhike so far, and all alone. But

he did suddenly appear doubtful, as if he were embarrassed that an innocent joke had been taken so seriously.
His smile disappeared, or almost.

"I don't know," he said dubiously. "I was planning to
start right now and drive all night. I'm afraid you'd get
too tired." •

"Oh, I don't mind that at all," Ellen said. "I've often
slept in my father's . . . I've often slept in cars."

"Well," said the young man, still sounding doubtful,
"I suppose you could sleep in the back seat. It's big
enough. And it's empty."

"Oh, *please!*" Ellen said. "I was worried about the
hitchhiking, because I'm not sure how you wave your
thumb. If I ride with you, I don't have to do it."

"That's no trick," said the young man, and he showed
her how to do it, waving his hand and thumb in a proper
hitchhiking arc, and turning his smile up even higher.
"You always want to smile when you hitchhike," he explained. At the end of the lesson he extended the hand to
her, and she shook hands with him, closing the bargain.

"All right," he said. "You've got a ride."

She climbed into the big blue car, into the front seat,
sat down beside him, and they drove off. In her lap she
held her handbag, her loaf of bread, and the two road
maps.

"I'm Arthur Gates," the young man said after a moment. "I'm a teacher. What's your name?"

She said, "Ellen Carroll. I'm going to Kentucky to
visit my aunt."

"Kentucky is four hundred miles long and two hundred miles wide. What *part* of Kentucky does your aunt

live in?"

"Near Lexington," Ellen said. "Near a village called Oakstable."

"You're in luck," Mr. Gates said. "I go right through Lexington." And his smile grew broader than ever.

In luck, indeed. Half an hour earlier Ellen had had only the vaguest idea of how she would get to the Blue Hill; now she was on her way in luxury; tomorrow she would be *there*. It was incredible luck.

Mr. Gates drove very fast, and not very skillfully, Ellen thought, so there was quite a lot of unnecessary slamming on of brakes and occasional screeching of tires. Still, in half an hour or so they were out of the city traffic. On the open highway there were very few cars, and in another hour they reached the first of the mountains.

Ellen loved mountains. The way the big car swung up the highway into them made her feel as if she were flying—as you feel on a sled, sometimes, when you come down a steep slope and zoom up another. She loved the forests that covered them, with hardly a house anywhere. The day was beautiful and sunny, and there was just enough wind to toss the leaves and make them sparkle in the sunlight. As they went higher, they drove through long miles of pine woods, from a distance a solid coat of green fur on the mountain's back, but up close, looking from the car window through the trees, an endless series of pillars growing up through dark, mysterious chambers with carpeted brown floors. The sight always made Ellen want to get out and walk through their shadowy corridors, heading up and up until she reached the top of the mountain, the only person for miles around.

Mr. Gates did not talk much. He seemed preoccupied, as if he were thinking about some private problem that had nothing to do with driving the car. And he had the oddest way, every now and then, of breaking into an absolutely delighted smile, so that Ellen kept expecting him to chuckle and tell her what it was about, but he never did.

At first Ellen herself thought she ought to try to make conversation, so she asked, more out of politeness than curiosity:

"What kind of a school do you teach in?"

Mr. Gates then did a very odd thing. He jumped, almost as if he had forgotten she was there; then he turned his head slightly, held out his right hand, and said:

"I'm Arthur Gates. I'm a teacher. What's your name?"

This was exactly what he had said before, when they first met, and it was said in precisely the same tones, as if he had memorized it. But before she could answer, Mr. Gates recovered, blinked his eyes, and his smile went away. He added quickly:

"You might call it a sort of training school for boys. Well, mostly boys, but now we're beginning to get a few girls, too." At that his smile returned, and grew bigger and happier than ever, but he did not say anything more. There was something very strange about him, Ellen decided, but it did not really matter. Whatever he was smiling about, he was taking her to Kentucky, and at a very fast clip, too.

She wondered how many miles they had come. She knew there was a dial on the dashboard that showed mileage, but she could not read it from where she sat. After a while she made up a sort of mile-game: where the road was straight enough she would pick out a land-mark—a big tree, a clump of pines, a cliff, a fence—that she guessed to be a mile ahead, and when, in a minute or so they *whooshed* past it, that was one more mile closer to the Blue Hill and Aunt Sarah.

The sun sank lower in the sky, the woods grew darker and more mysterious, and Ellen began to feel sleepy. She also felt hungry again and remembered the sandwich remaining in her pocket. She also remembered to be polite. She took out the sandwich, broke it in two, and said to Mr. Gates:

"Would you like half my sandwich? It's peanut butter and jam."

This time Mr. Gates responded quite normally. "No, thank you," he said. "I ate just before we left. I don't plan to eat again until we're there." Well, *almost* normally; "until we're there" sounded to Ellen as if he were going to Aunt Sarah's, too, or at least as if they were both going to the same place, and they weren't really. What he meant, of course, must be "until we get to Kentucky."

She munched the sandwich. It had grown stale; the peanut butter stuck to the top of her mouth, and she realized she was quite thirsty. Whenever she had taken a trip with her family, they had always taken along a bottle of water, or milk in a thermos, or cokes in an ice-bucket, because somebody was forever getting thirsty. But there was no bottle anywhere to be seen in Mr. Gates's car. In fact, it was as empty and shiny as if he had just bought it.

So she finished her dry sandwich and then, suddenly, she was asleep.

She slept as the dark came on, as Mr. Gates turned on the headlights and the big car hurtled through the night like a bright-eyed blue beetle droning its narrow way through the miles of black trees. She came only half awake once, when Mr. Gates stopped the car at a filling station and bought gas; she had a vague impression that he also made a telephone call. She slept in the front seat, not the back, scrunched over in the corner.

She did not know how late it was, nor how long she had been asleep, when she was awakened by a loud squealing of brakes, a long and frightening screech of the tires; the car swung fiercely from side to side as it skidded, and then stopped so abruptly that she was thrown forward and hit her head hard on the dashboard. Ahead of them, just a few inches from the headlights, a truck had run partly off the highway; it lay at an odd angle, its left rear wheels up in the air like a tilted elephant's feet, its front wheels in the ditch. The trailer's rear doors had sprung open, and there were boxes and cartons lying all over the road. The trailer itself was blocking half the highway, and they had come within a foot of crashing into it.

Ellen scarcely glanced at all this. When she bumped her head, the blow made her see at first a bright flash of light. It vanished, but there still remained a softer light directly in front of her eyes, and now she saw why: she had struck her head on the button that snaps the glove compartment shut. It had fallen open, and a small light had turned on, illuminating its interior.

When Mr. Gates saw this he reached over very quickly and slammed it shut. But not before Ellen saw lying inside the compartment a pistol with a long barrel she recognized instantly, and a shimmering green hood with two eyeholes staring vacantly up at her.

The Flight into the Forest

MR. GATES'S long arm reached out as Ellen opened the car door; his hand clawed at her as she slid from the seat; it closed so hard that his thumb and fingers met through the paper wrapping of the loaf of bread, which was all that he caught. Ellen was out of the car and into the black pine woods.

The forest was a bottomless lake of the blackest India ink. Ellen ran with her hands outstretched in front of her face. She slithered, slid and scurried, heading uphill, diving around the great scaly trunks when her fingers touched them. Her feet slipped on the carpet of pine needles, which muffled her footsteps and kept her progress secret. They did the same for Mr. Gates, however, who was instantly through the door in pursuit.

In this deadly race Ellen soon realized she had one advantage: she was short. The pine branches spread horizontally from the boles beginning at about five feet; the

33

top of Ellen's head, at 55½ inches, cleared most of them neatly. Mr. Gates who was much taller would have to bend forward. This evidently threw him off balance, for Ellen heard him falling occasionally, and sometimes crashing into tree trunks. Within a few minutes he was panting so loudly that she could hear quite easily where he was all the time. He had run farther to the left than she had and was now, she guessed, a couple of hundred feet away.

She ran a little farther and then stopped. If she could hear his breathing, then he would hear hers, if she ran too hard. She lay down on the ground and pressed her face into her hands and into the soft pine carpet, trying to breathe as gently as possible. After a while Mr. Gates seemed to realize he was giving his position away; at any rate she no longer heard him crashing about, and in a few minutes his puffing stopped. In all the dark woods there was not a sound. Even the wind had died.

She lay absolutely still, hoping that the forest was big enough so that he would miss her. Was he standing still, listening, or was he searching, silently now, creeping through the dark?

A few minutes passed and then she heard a noise, a dry rasping like two dead leaves rubbing together. It was Mr. Gates's hand, touching the piney scales of a tr trunk as he felt his way forward. Now she heard his breath again, very softly, like the faintest of whispers. He could not be more than six feet away. It was too late to get up and run; instead she tried to make herself completely rigid, and she held her breath. The whisper came closer. She heard a muffled footstep, and then his hard, heavy shoe came down on her ankle, crushing it so that she thought it would snap, and the pain shot all the way up to her face. Still she did not move, nor breathe, and for once there was an advantage in being thin, for Mr. Gates either did not feel her small bone underfoot, or, more likely, thought it was only a pine bough. In a second or so he lifted his foot, took another step, and crept on.

When he had passed she let the air from her lungs out slowly, and inhaled again, working hard not to gasp. Just as she did this he began calling, very gently. He was perhaps twenty feet away.

"Ellen?" And again: "Ellen?" He said it sweetly, affectionately, as if she were his own daughter, lost in the night. His voice was so high it sounded as if he were singing.

"Ellen, please come out," the clear voice called. "I'm not going to hurt you. We've got to go on to Kentucky now."

A pause. No sound at all. Then once more: "Ellen, don't you want to see your Aunt Sarah? I'm going to take you right to her house. You can be with her tomorrow morning. We're almost there. Please, Ellen, let's go on. You can't stay here alone in the woods."

All this was spoken in the kindliest, most concerned voice, but there was one very odd thing about it. Ellen was almost certain that she had never told him her aunt's name. Yet how else could he possibly have known? She lay still, pressed against the ground.

Something must have moved, however, or at least Mr. Gates thought something did—perhaps some small animal, frightened by his calling.

In any case he gave a shout, and she heard him pounce and crash to the ground. Then he was off again, running blindly through the woods, chasing something he thought was Ellen, but moving now away from her, down the hillside. She took advantage of the noise to move, carefully and quietly, another hundred feet in the opposite direction, up the hill.

After a few minutes Mr. Gates stopped again, quite far away, so that she could hardly hear his panting. Once more he shouted into the woods, but this time in the strangest way, saying things that made no sense to Ellen at all. There was nothing sweet about his voice now. He was screaming.

"Ellen." High and shrill. "You must come out. I *order* you to come out. The King has commanded me to bring you to him. The King himself has ordered it. You must come." Then, like a chant: "You *will* come. You *will* come. You *will* come. If you don't come now, you will come later." More silence, and then the same again. "You *will* come, or we will be punished."

But when he spoke again, for the last time, he was no longer talking to Ellen, but to himself, in a whimper. "*I* will be punished. They will put me in the . . ." Was it *machine* he said? Or *screen*? Ellen could not be sure, for at the word his voice broke entirely and turned into a weak, bubbling wail. Mr. Gates was hysterical. Still wailing, he blundered his way down the hill, and in a little while she heard the car start in the distance; the engine roared, the tires screamed terribly, and he drove off.

Ellen climbed a little higher up the mountain, found

a level spot, and sat down. The night was cool but not cold; the pine carpet under her gave off warmth it had collected during the day, and was as soft as a mattress. In a few minutes she lay back and fell asleep from exhaustion.

She was free of Mr. Gates, but free she knew not where, in a wilderness with no food or drink. She had only her pocketbook left, looped fast around her wrist.

While she slept, she had a nightmare. She stood in the throne room of her castle, which she recognized instantly although it had been changed. The dais where the throne used to stand had been made much larger and higher, and turned into a stage. Onstage there was a hideous performance going on. Twenty boys and young men, all wearing green hoods, were attacking a policeman, who stood defenseless, dressed in blue, in the center. First five from the left, armed with clubs and knives, would dart in and circle the policeman like Indians, stabbing and beating viciously. Then, all together, they would slink away and another five (from the right) would take their places. It was gracefully and swiftly done, like a ballet, but all in complete silence. The policeman, she finally realized, was not real. He was a dummy, a sort of practice policeman, hung from the ceiling by a rope around his neck, so that his head dangled off to one side. Now she saw that in a pit in front of the stage there was a director, positioned so low that only the top of the back of his head was visible. He wore a crown exactly like hers, except that it was black.

Otto the Wrecker *

ELLEN was awakened by a flock of crows sitting in a circle in a treetop high above her. They were talking. From having lived for many years in the country, Ellen knew that crows can say a great deal more than just "caw." That raucous cry, in fact, is only a warning signal; it means "watch out," or, in a different tone, "help." But left to themselves on a quiet morning, crows will conduct whole conversations in quiet voices, talking one at a time. That is what these were doing now, and Ellen thought she could even distinguish the leader-crow, setting forth the plans for the day.

Anyway, it was a gentle way to wake up, and when Ellen moved, a squirrel scurried up a tree a few feet away, darting around to the back side of the trunk to hide from her. Like most squirrels, he did not know how long

* One who searches for, or works upon, the wrecks of vessels, etc., as for rescue or for plunder.—Webster's New Collegiate Dictionary.

his tail was, and left it sticking out, so she was able to watch that much of him all the way up until he vanished into the thick green pine needles.

Above the needles the sun was shining, but down at the bottom of the forest only a few bright spears found their way, moving like slow searchlights across the ground as the sun rose higher.

Ellen sat up. She was terribly thirsty; she was also hungry, but in a battle between thirst and hunger, thirst always wins. Her forehead was bruised where she had bumped the dashboard, and the ankle Mr. Gates had stepped on was sore and swollen a little. But mainly she was thirsty.

Somewhere in this woods, she thought, there must be a brook; and suddenly the idea of a brook with cold water running over stones seemed like the most delicious thought she had ever had. It made her twice as thirsty as before. But it also occurred to her that a surer way to find water might be to find the highway again, because somewhere along the roadside, sooner or later, there would be a house where she could knock on the door and ask for a drink.

She was sure she could find the road. Since in leaving it she had run uphill all the way, to find it she had merely to walk downhill. So she set off, keeping a sharp eye out for a brook and another for Mr. Gates, though for some reason she felt quite certain he was really gone.

She walked for perhaps ten minutes, limping slightly, thinking about Mr. Gates. When she had seen the gun and the green hood, she had known immediately that he was the one who had shot the store manager and poor

Officer Drogue. There was, she realized now, something about the way he moved that should have reminded her of the murderer immediately. But she had been so eager to get the ride to Kentucky that she had not paid attention.

She wondered, too, about his knowing Aunt Sarah's name. *Perhaps* she had told him, but she did not think so. And then there was that strange thing Officer Drogue had said before he ran off—"another green hood." It all added up to a puzzle she could not solve.

She saw no brook, and the road seemed farther away than she had thought. But suddenly, right in front of her, she saw something she recognized.

It was not the road, but it was *from* the road. It was a stack of brown cardboard cartons, piled neatly behind a very large tree trunk. And behind another trunk nearby stood another stack. They were, she was quite sure, some of the same cartons that had fallen out of the wrecked truck the night before. There must have been ten or more of them piled up. But how had they gotten here?

She walked over to one of the stacks and looked at the top carton. Stencilled in black letters on one end were the words, "Blue Ridge Apple Juice—One Doz."

Apple juice. She loved it, and right now she felt she could drink the whole box. She was pulling the carton off the pile when the thought struck her, it's not my apple juice. It belongs to somebody. I can't just take it. And then she thought, I'll just drink one bottle, and I'll wait here; when the owner comes I'll pay him for it from my money. If the owner did not come soon, she could simply leave a quarter on top of the carton. That would surely be enough for one bottle.

She lifted the heavy box to the ground, pulled the top open, and took out a bottle. Sure enough, there was the juice, gurgling deliciously inside the brown glass. But how was she to get the top off without a bottle opener? She picked up a stick and pried at it, but the stick broke. She stood up and looked around for a better tool—a pointed rock, maybe.

Not six feet away, a small boy stood, barefooted, watching her with wary brown eyes. In his hand he held a very large hunting knife. He held it out to her politely, handle first. He said:

"Here. Open it with this."

"Is it yours?"

"Yes. That is, it fell off a truck. When they hauled the truck away this morning, they left these boxes. But you can have some."

"Why didn't they take them?"

"I don't know. I guess they were in the ditch where they couldn't see them." His eyes looked away. "They were in a hurry to move the truck."

Ellen took the knife and pried the top loose. She drained half the bottle without stopping.

"Gee," said the boy. "You must be thirsty."

"I am. I've been thirsty ever since yesterday."

"Do you want some water? Water's better when you're thirsty."

"I know. I couldn't find any."

"I know where there's some."

"Where?"

"Right up here. Come on."

He led the way, and in a few steps, just out of sight of
the boxes, they came to a large, flat-topped boulder, over
the top of which trickled the clearest, cleanest, coldest-
looking spring in the world. It ran down the side of the
rock into a tiny pool, from which someone had raked
away the pine needles, leaving a sparkling bed of rock
and sand.

She lay down and drank the icy water until she felt
dizzy.

"You don't want to drink too fast when you're thirsty,"
the boy warned.

"I know. I'll stop now. What's your name?"

"Otto. There was a man up on the hill last night, chasing somebody."

"I know. He was chasing me. Did you hear him?"

"No, I was asleep in bed. I saw his tracks. I saw yours,
too. You were here all night?" He really did not mean it
as a question; he knew. "Where'd the man go?"

"He drove away. I *guess*. At least I heard his car."

"That's what I thought. I saw where he ran back to
the road. He sure fell down a lot."

He certainly seemed to know a great deal, considering
how small he was. He was dressed in worn-out gray
trousers, ragged at the ankles, patched at the knees, and
a faded cotton flannel shirt which had once been blue
plaid. His coal black hair was cut straight all around. But
except for his bare feet, which were stained brown, he
looked clean and rather nice. Ellen liked him.

"How old are you?" she asked.

He looked embarrassed. "About eight and a half, I
think."

"You mean you don't *know*?" Ellen asked in amazement.

"Well, not exactly. My mother says I was born in the fall, she thinks maybe October, but she can't remember for sure. She's so old, she forgets lot of things."

"But your *birthday* . . ."

"Oh, I have a birthday, all right."

"Well, when is it?"

"When we get stuff for a birthday cake, in the fall, then we have my birthday," he said patiently, as if he were explaining something simple to a simpleton. He clearly disliked the whole subject, so he changed it.

"What's your name?"

"Ellen Carroll."

"How old are you?"

"Ten. My birthday was yesterday." She started to tell him about the crown, then decided against it, but felt her pocketbook to make sure it was still there. It was.

"What's in the pocketbook?"

"Oh, things. Doesn't your father know when your birthday is?" Ellen changed the subject back again.

"I don't have any father."

"Oh. I'm sorry," Ellen said. "Did he die?"

"No. He just left. We didn't care. We didn't like him anyway. We don't want him back."

He stood up. "I've got to take these boxes up to my house."

"All of them?"

"Well, not all at once." (Patiently again.) "I carry one at a time."

"Where's your house?"

"Up there." He pointed. "About a mile. It takes all day to get a bunch like this up there. I got eleven this time." He had an afterthought.

"Are you lost?"

"No. At least, not really." But the truth was, Ellen realized for the first time, she was lost. "That is, I don't know where I am."

"Then you're lost. That's what being lost *is*." He added: "Look, you better come with me. You can talk to my mother."

When Ellen thought about it, she realized that she had little choice. She had lost her food and her road maps; she had no idea how far Mr. Gates had driven her, nor even, really, whether he had gone toward Kentucky at all. Otto's mother, being a grownup, would know where she was and in which direction Kentucky lay.

"All right. I'll carry one of the boxes," she said.

They set out. Ellen carried the carton of apple juice. Otto lifted another to his shoulder. It said, "Dried Split Peas—2 lbs.—1 doz."

Both boxes were heavy, but Otto carried his lightly; his small shoulders were straight and sturdy. But Ellen had trouble. In a hundred yards or so the hard cardboard surface of the carton had found a knuckle in her shoulder bone and was rasping it unbearably. She put it down, switched it to the other shoulder, and then trotted through the trees to catch up with Otto, who had not paused. In a few minutes the same thing happened to the other shoulder. Then she tried carrying it like a baby, in both arms, and that was better except that, unlike a baby, it was slippery and kept sliding down. Also, the extra weight made her sore ankle hurt.

Finally, out of breath, she called: "Can we stop and rest a minute?"

Otto stopped. To his credit, he was not scornful, but only slightly superior, and even a little sympathetic.

"Girls aren't very strong," he said, "but mainly you aren't used to it. Some of the stuff I carry up is twice this heavy. Once I got an armchair. *That* was *hard*." Ellen could imagine him, like an ant with a watermelon seed, toiling an armchair up the hill.

"I don't understand," she said, panting as she sank to the ground. "Have other trucks wrecked here, too, before last night?"

"All the time. One every three, four months, sometimes more. There's a bad grade, with a bend that hides it."

"But that's so dangerous. Why don't they fix it?"

"It's not really *too* dangerous. Nobody's ever got hurt yet. They all do the same thing—front of the cab goes in the ditch, front of the trailer goes in the air, stuff falls out the back. Driver gets out and walks for help."

"But suppose the driver gets hurt?"

"They never do."

"But he might."

"Then I guess I'd have to go for help."

"What about the boxes?"

"Well, what about them?"

"Do they always fall in the ditch?"

Otto looked evasive again. "Well, usually. But it's not always boxes. One time it was live chickens, in those wire cages—we still have some chickens left from that one. One time it was light bulbs, hundreds and hundreds of them. We couldn't use them, because we've got no electricity; mostly they broke, anyway, and there was glass all over the road."

"But is it all right . . . I mean, are you allowed to just take them like this?"

Otto's tanned face turned dark red, as if Ellen had hit him. He was suddenly furious.

"I've *got* to take them. I've *got* to. My mother is old, and she hardly has any money. When I get bigger, I can earn money, but I can't now. And in the winter I have to go to school, anyway. If no trucks wreck, we don't have anything to eat."

He stood up. "Come on. I've got to get this home."

"I'm sorry," Ellen said. "I didn't mean to make you feel bad. I think you're right. I really do."

But Otto's anger was already gone. He helped her lift the carton of apple juice, then shouldered his own box. "Come on," he said again. "It's only a little way more."

And in a few minutes they came to a dirt road, a wagon track, leading up the hill from the highway. They rounded a bend into a clearing, and there Ellen saw a small, pretty, white house surrounded by gardens, both flower and vegetable. In one of them a tall woman in a long gray dress was working with a hoe.

Richard

OTTO'S mother, whose name was Mrs. Fitzpatrick, welcomed Ellen pleasantly, and without any particular surprise; as if Otto were always bringing things home from the forest, and this time it was a girl. Otto said:

"Mother, she was lost in the woods. A man chased her last night, and she doesn't even know where she is."

"Otto," said his mother, putting down her hoe and peering at Ellen, "the girl is not only lost. She is exhausted, frightened, hungry, lonely, and she has been through a disaster. And who knows what more? Her ankle is swollen—and her carrying a heavy box like that. Put it down, child."

And Ellen did.

"Now, dear, come into the house, and we'll get you some breakfast. We'll have sausage and eggs and biscuits, and how about some nice fresh peaches with powdered sugar on them?"

47

This sounded so good to Ellen that it made her head spin, and she stumbled as she followed Mrs. Fitzpatrick into the house.

Mrs. Fitzpatrick seemed to Ellen to be too old to be the mother of a young boy like Otto. She looked more like a grandmother. Her face was brown and gnarled and wrinkled, like a pumpkin-sized walnut. She was tall, her hair was pure gray, and despite her years she stood as straight as her hoe handle. Her dress was threadbare but elegantly simple; it reached all the way to her ankles, and looked as if she had made it herself.

She could cook. The sausage was the tenderest, spiciest, sweetest, meatiest Ellen had ever tasted; the eggs, before they were cooked, were still warm from the hen; the biscuits were brown and white, crispy, soft, crumbly and crunchy all at the same time. Ellen ate three eggs, four pieces of sausage, five biscuits (they were small) and a big bowl of sliced peaches with sugar on them.

After she had eaten all she could, Mrs. Fitzpatrick took her hand and led her to a small, cheerful room at the back of the house. It had a sunny window looking out at a peach tree, a pretty rocking chair, and a bed with a plain blue cotton coverlet.

"We've not used this room for a long time," said Mrs. Fitzpatrick. "It is your room, now, for as long as you need it. I know you have had a terrible and sad time, and you had very little sleep last night, for your face looks lost and desperate, and your eyes have black shadows under them as big as cucumbers. You must sleep, or you will be ill."

So Ellen lay down on the bed, with her shoes off and

her head on the pillow, and Mrs. Fitzpatrick sat for a moment beside her and looked at her with a most kindly and compassionate expression.

"Poor little Ellen," she said. "I do not know that your trouble is over, but you are safe here, for a time at least." And she put her gnarled, strong hand on Ellen's head and stroked her hair. Then she left, closing the door behind her.

Ellen had had, for the past twenty-four hours and more, a well in her throat and a wrench in her stomach, which, since she was of royal blood, she had held back by clamping her chin and holding it up high. But now that small touch on her hair pressed her chin down, and the well burst and the Queen sobbed a huge sob and then cried, hard and bitterly, at last. Luckily there was no one there to see, since Mrs. Fitzpatrick had left the room.

"What is happening to me? My house burned, my family are all killed, Officer Drogue is killed, Mr. Gates is a murderer and chased me through the woods. But he did not even know me. Except, somehow, maybe he did, since he knew Aunt Sarah's name. And he acted so strange, and at the end, really crazy." She remembered Mr. Gates's high, terrified wail as he ran back to the car, crashing and falling. Ellen felt as if she were being blown along with no control over her direction by some irresistible, angry hurricane; yet a personal kind of a hurricane nonetheless, designed especially for her, and one which knew where it was going though she did not. With this horrifying thought she fell asleep, and, oddly enough, did not dream at all.

When she woke up the afternoon sun was shining in

the window. She put her shoes back on, shaking some
pine needles out of them first, and went to the door. She
could not open it; it was locked. Why? She shook the
knob, knocked, and listened. There was no sound in the
house. Then, quickly, she dashed to the window. Directly outside of it sat Otto, under the peach tree, on the
last of the cartons from the truck. He saw her at the
window, and made a motion for her to open it. She did.

"Shhh," he whispered. "Don't move."

Ellen stayed where she was, wondering. Then Otto
whistled. An answering whistle came from the leaves of
the peach tree.

"Richard," said Otto.

"Richard," said the tree in a squawky voice.

"Richard come."

"Richard come," said the tree, and a shiny, blue-black
crow fluttered onto Otto's shoulder.

"Good Richard," said Otto.

"Good Richard," squawked the crow. "Good Richard
eat. Richard eat, Richard eat, eat, eat." Otto took a biscuit from his pocket, crumbled it in his palm and held it
out. The crow gobbled it greedily, murmuring, "Richard
eat" in a doughy voice after each bite. Then it flew back
into the tree.

Ellen was impressed. "How did he learn to talk?"

"I taught him. I found him in the woods when he was
a baby. He couldn't fly, so I put him in a box in my
room. I fed him worms and bread and bugs. And berries.
He'll eat anything."

"Can he talk more than that?"

"Sure. He can say a lot of things. And he's still learning. Come on out."

"I can't. The door's locked."

"I know. My mother locked it. Come out the window."

Since it was a first-floor window, Ellen scrambled out easily enough and stood beside Otto under the tree.

"Why did she lock me in?"

"I think she was locking everybody else out," Otto said. "She had to go out in the garden. I think she didn't like leaving you alone. Anyway, she told me to watch your window."

"I wonder why."

"I don't know. I guess because of that man that chased you."

"But he's gone."

"But he might come back."

"How would he know I'm here?"

"I don't know. He might find out."

Ellen looked around apprehensively and shivered slightly.

"Oh, he's not around here now," Otto said.

"How do you know? He might be hiding in the trees."

"Richard would know. Crows have terrific eyes. Ears, too. If any strangers come near here, he makes a terrible squawking noise, and he won't come down out of the tree."

"I'm a stranger."

"Yes, but you came with me."

"He's like a watch dog."

"Better. He can fly up in the air and see a mile."

"Gee," Ellen said, feeling relieved. "That's smart."

"There's one thing wrong with him, though. He's no

good at night. He just sleeps in the tree, won't fly, won't talk, won't anything."

Just then Richard came fluttering down again, not quite to Otto's shoulder this time, since he was shy of Ellen, but to a low branch.

"Richard," he said again. "Richard eat." But Otto had no more food in his pockets, so in a moment the crow took off with a whir of wings, heading toward the woods and calling out what sounded to Ellen like "oughter, oughter, oughter."

"What's he saying?"

"He means *water*. Come on. I'll show you." And Otto scrambled off after the crow, with Ellen following.

They walked—Otto ran ahead, but Ellen still limped, so he slowed and waited for her—uphill, into the woods behind the house. This was not pine forest, but great, wide-branching oak trees, growing just the right distance apart so that each massive trunk seemed to stand in its own house, with its own high ceiling of boughs and leaves. Above and ahead of them Ellen could glimpse Richard fluttering from branch to branch. He had slowed down for her, too.

At length she heard ahead of them a gentle soughing, a murmur, then a gurgling—a brook. And they stepped out onto the bank of a pond. But what a pond! It looked like the enchanted pool in a fairy tale, because it was perfectly round, about the size of a large room, with a curved rock cliff walling it in on one end, and a tiny new moon of a sandy beach on the other. Through the sand into the pond bubbled the brook Ellen had heard.

She stood staring in delight until Otto, who had been

rolling up his pant-legs, sprang through the air with a
shout and landed ankle-deep at the sandy end of the
pool. Then he kicked a big splash of water at Ellen,
spattering her from head to foot.

"Don't," said Ellen, covering her face. But she couldn't
help laughing; the water felt lovely on her face, and in a
minute she had kicked off her shoes and joined Otto in
the pond.

"Can you swim?" he asked.

"Some. Not too well."

"Be careful, then. The other end is deep."

"How deep?"

"Watch." He picked up from the bank a long, straight
branch, twice as tall as he was. Moving from the shallow
sandy end where the brook came in, he waded until he
was up to his knees—about halfway across. Then, reaching as far forward as he could, he thrust the branch
straight down. It disappeared beneath the water without
touching bottom; a moment later it appeared on the surface again, and Otto caught it and threw it back on the
bank.

"You see? It drops off, just like a cliff. No bottom from
here on to the rock."

"You could dive off the rock."

"I do. I wish we had our bathing suits."

"I don't have a bathing suit," Ellen said. "I don't have
any clothes besides these."

"My mother will make you some," Otto said. "She can
sew anything. She's got whole batches of cloth."

"From a truck?"

"From a truck," Otto said cheerfully. "Watch out!"

Ellen ducked, as with a piercing shriek Richard dive-bombed them both from a limb above and glided like a black jet to a landing on the beach.

"Oh," said Ellen in sudden alarm. "Has he seen someone?"

"No. He's just mad at me."

"What for? He scared me."

"Because I'm talking to you."

"He's jealous?"

"No. He wants a fish. I'll show you."

There were schools of small, light brown minnows swimming in the shallow water, chasing their gray shadows across the sand. Otto picked up the same long stick and waded toward the shallow end near the brook, watching his feet and pushing the stick sideways toward shore. By doing this he herded one school of little fish toward the beach. At the last minute most of them turned and darted under the stick, around his legs, and got away. But a few swam to the edge and beached themselves in an inch of water. Otto leaped over the stick, plunged his hands down, and came up with a wriggling minnow in each fist.

Richard, who had been watching all this calmly with a bright black eye, now turned slightly in the sand, balancing himself on his toes, and said, "Eat." He did not fly to Otto's shoulder, and Ellen saw why.

Otto, with a careful underhand toss, sent a fish arching and wriggling through the air. With a quick, deft stretch of his neck Richard caught it in the air and swallowed it in one gulp. The other followed a second later.

"That's *neat*," Ellen said. "But the poor little fish."

"They don't mind."

"How do you know?"

"They're too dumb. They don't feel anything."

"But how do you know? They might."

"Don't you eat fish?"

"Well, sometimes. But not much."

"You eat bacon. Pigs feel things. They squeal like murder."

Ellen was learning that Otto was, among other things, a merciless opponent in argument.

"I've never heard them," she said rather lamely. And she resolved firmly, for about ten seconds, never to eat bacon—or fish—again.

So they talked, and argued, and waded and sat on the sand in the sun until the shadows of the big trees crept across and covered the pool.

"We've got to go home," Otto said at last. "I've got to bring in the wood."

"The wood?"

"For the stove. To cook dinner."

Ellen did not argue about that. She was hungry. But she had never seen a stove that used wood.

A Cry in the Night

IN the middle of Mrs. Fitzpatrick's house there was one big, cluttered, comfortable, rectangular chamber that served as kitchen, dining and living room combined. Her wood stove was the biggest object in it. It was made of velvet-black cast iron; it had six round stovelids as big as pies, and an oven big enough to hold a grown man (if properly folded); it stood on six shiny legs and was studded with gleaming nickel-plated knobs and spring-wire handles to regulate the draughts and open and close the doors. Its firebox had a glass window, so you could see the glowing logs inside. Out over the whole thing curved a great metal hood, with wide shelves to put things on to keep them warm, and above that, like a single huge organ stop, rose the stovepipe, curving majestically up and into the chimney.

The smells that came out of it were just as beautiful: the smell of cloves and ham, of roasting sweet potatoes, of fresh bread, and piercing through all of these, of a sweet cake baking.

At the stove end of the room, near a window, stood a plain wooden trestle table with benches along the sides and a chair at the end.

The other end of the room was lined with bookshelves, and books stood on them all the way to the ceiling. There were blue books, brown books, green ones and black ones, but most notably they were all old books, except for a few on an end of one of the lower shelves. These were children's books that Otto had acquired one way or another.

At this end of the room there was an old but comfortable sofa, several wooden chairs, a window seat with potted flowers growing on it and a cushion to sit on, and a big, rather ugly new armchair. At one end of the sofa stood a lamp table with a pretty, old-fashioned kerosene lamp on it. The mate of this lamp, which had a flowery white shade, stood on the dining table. A third hung from the ceiling near the stove. As evening fell and dinnertime came, Mrs. Fitzpatrick lit all three of these with a match. They gave off a pleasant, warm yellow light, much nicer than electric bulbs.

Perhaps, as Otto had said, Mrs. Fitzpatrick did not have much money now, but she obviously had had some once. Because when Ellen said, as her mother had taught her, "May I help?", Mrs. Fitzpatrick smiled and said, "You may set the table, if you like." And she led Ellen to the cabinet where the table-setting things were kept. Her knives, spoons and forks were heavy, antique sterling silver, and there were a great many of them, all stored in a velvet-lined box of silver-inlaid wood—not the kind of

things any poor bride would have had. Her tablecloths
and napkins, too, were of fine, heavy damask. And none
of these, obviously, had come from a wrecked truck, since
both linens and silver bore on each piece the same mono-
gram, in Old English—or Old Irish—letters: "FP."

Ellen's dinner was even better than the meal she had
had before. After they had finished eating, Mrs. Fitzpatrick pushed back her chair and said:

"Now we will clean up the dishes, and then, Ellen, you
must tell me your story, everything that has happened to
you, so we can decide whether you are still in danger, and
what you should do next."

Half an hour later they sat in the other end of the room,
Mrs. Fitzpatrick on the sofa next to the lamp, Otto next
to her, and Ellen in the armchair, which was comfortable
despite being ugly. They made an odd little group, sitting
there in the golden lamplight in the house in the dark
woods.

"Now," said Mrs. Fitzpatrick, "begin at the beginning."

"I will," said Ellen. "It began yesterday morning at
seven o'clock. I woke up in my room, and it was my
birthday."

"Begin a little before that," said Mrs. Fitzpatrick, "and
tell me where you lived, and about your family."

So Ellen did that, and then came back to the morning
of her birthday, and told about going to the park, and
hearing the fire engines, and running back, and about
the fireman and Officer Drogue. She told about the shooting at the store, and the green hood and the strange thing
Officer Drogue had said before he ran off.

"You're sure that's what he said?" asked Mrs. Fitzpatrick. "*Another* green hood?"

"Yes," said Ellen. "But he wasn't saying it to me. He was saying it to himself."

"But you yourself had not seen anyone in a green hood before."

"Well . . ." said Ellen, and then she remembered something she had forgotten until this moment. "When I first started from the house, I remember now, I thought I saw somebody down the block, and I thought he had a green face. But then I decided it was just some leaves. It was misty."

Mrs. Fitzpatrick's expression now became less puzzled and more grim. Otto was listening raptly. But since neither of them said anything more, Ellen continued her story. She told about the fat man, and the postcard, and Mr. Gates, and about running away from him through the woods, and all the rest, up to meeting Otto.

Yet there was one strange thing: At first without realizing it, and then, realizing it, purposely, she carefully avoided even mentioning the silver crown. She did not know why.

She had an odd feeling that perhaps it should be kept a secret. She kept thinking that when she got to the end, then she could tell about the crown. But when she had got to the end, she was still undecided, so she said nothing.

Mrs. Fitzpatrick, however, seemed to see a hole in a story as clearly as a hole in a windowpane. She looked at Ellen with her sharp gray eyes, and shook her head.

"You have not told it all," she said. "Your story does not ring true. Some piece of it is missing. I can sense it. I cannot help you unless you tell me everything that happened. Now think hard. You have forgotten something. Something important. What?"

Ellen looked at the floor. She was ashamed.

"I didn't forget anything. I just didn't tell it all. I'm sorry. But I will now." Her mind was finally made up; she went to the bedroom she had slept in and got her handbag from under the pillow, where she had left it when she climbed out the window. She carried it back to the living room. She took out the silver crown, its stones glittering like blue snowflakes in the lamplight, and put it on her head.

"This is what I didn't tell," she said. "It's a crown I got for my birthday."

It was Otto who spoke first. He had drawn back, as if in fright, at the sight of the crown, and when he spoke his voice was full of awe.

"It's *magical*," he said to Mrs. Fitzpatrick, almost whispering. "It makes her look different—like somebody else."

Mrs. Fitzpatrick said, "No. Not like somebody else. Like herself, but more like herself than most people can ever look."

"I don't understand," said Otto; and Ellen, who had been about to say the same thing, kept still.

"Nor do I," said Mrs. Fitzpatrick. "At least not entirely. But I think that I have heard of this crown before. In fact, if it is the crown I believe it is, then it is quite famous—though that is not to say that its fame is known to a very large number of people.

"And magical is not exactly the right word for it, unless by magic you mean simply something you do not understand. And if that's all you mean, why then almost everything is magical."

And to Ellen she said, "Now I begin to understand a little of your story. And I will give you some advice: you had an instinct, a feeling, that the crown should be kept secret. You were right. From now on, show it to no one and tell no one about it unless you are sure he is your friend—much surer than you are of me. Although I am your friend, and will try to help you, I might have been deceiving you. And there are those who would deceive you, and even kill you, to get it from you.

"And now tell me, who gave it to you?"

"I don't know," said Ellen. And she told how she had found it lying on her pillow when she awoke. "I just thought it was a present, but I didn't think about how it got there. I just thought it was mine."

"And so it is," said Mrs. Fitzpatrick. "That much is obvious at a glance." She thought for a few minutes, then asked: "This Aunt Sarah you spoke about—did she ever mention this crown? Or any crown?"

"No," said Ellen, wondering, trying hard to remember. She added with some embarrassment, "But she did tell me that I was truly a queen, and I didn't need just to pretend I was."

"And so you are," said Mrs. Fitzpatrick. "But queen of where? Queen of what? That is what we must find out. Or rather, that is what *you* must find out. I am afraid I cannot help you much in that. Only a few can wear this crown; and I am not one of them."

"Oh, but you may if you want to." Ellen took it off and held it out to her.

"True, I can put it on. But it would have no such effect

on me as it does on you."

"I don't understand."

"Nor do I, not well enough to explain it to you." She went to one of the bookshelves, high up, where some of the oldest, mustiest volumes stood, and took one down.

"There is something I must read, if I can find it," she said. "And it's time for you to go to bed. Ellen, I found something for you in one of the closets." And she opened the door and produced a soft blue flannel nightgown just Ellen's size. It was odd that she happened to have it, but it was lucky for Ellen, who had slept all the last night in her clothes.

Before she went to her room, Ellen said, "There's something else I remembered I didn't tell you. When I wrote to Aunt Sarah, I told her about the crown in the postcard."

"I'm glad of that," said Mrs. Fitzpatrick, "because we do know that she is your friend. I am sure she, too, knows something about the crown, and if she has received your postcard, you may be sure that she is worrying about you and it, and probably searching for you right now."

Then she added, rather grimly, "The trouble is, others are searching for you, too. We must be sure they don't find you first."

Ellen put on her nightgown, hanging her clothes carefully on a hanger to get at least some of the wrinkles out, for she would have to wear them again tomorrow. She got into bed and was asleep in three minutes.

It was the darkest part of the night when Ellen woke up in her bed. Something was wrong, something had awakened her, but she did not know what. She lay still, huddled under the covers, listening. The room was utterly black, the window only a shade of gray lighter. She could scarcely tell any difference when she opened her eyes and closed them. Now she heard it: a faint, oh-so-quiet rustling coming from—the window?—no, from outside the window, which she had left partly open. Someone or something was moving, close to the house.

Ellen began to tremble, and made herself stop. Should she run to the window, slam it shut and lock it? Should she run from the room and wake Mrs. Fitzpatrick? What she wanted most was to pull the covers over her head and lie still, and hope it was just a prowling stray dog; but she knew it was not; it was too stealthy, too carefully quiet.

Then the problem was solved for her. Whatever it was outside seemed to go suddenly mad, for there came through the window a raucous, terrifying burst of insane, shrieking laughter. She thought immediately of Mr. Gates. Now she did pull the covers over her head.

Her door opened; she heard brisk footsteps through the room, and heard Mrs. Fitzpatrick whisper, "Lie still. Don't move." She uncovered her eyes enough to see the pale gray rectangle of the window, the dim shadow of Mrs. Fitzpatrick holding something in her arms, then a bright white flash. There was a shattering roar, as if the whole room were exploding. Something thudded to the ground outside, and then there came the sound of heavy footsteps, someone running away from the house. Mrs. Fitzpatrick moved slightly; the flash and roar came again, and the footsteps doubled in speed. In the dimness of the window Ellen could see the pale gleam of something long and blue: Mrs. Fitzpatrick was holding a double-barreled shotgun.

"Whoever it was," she said, "he's gone now."

"Who was it?" Ellen asked.

"Someone looking for you, I expect." Mrs. Fitzpatrick opened the gun at the breech, took out the two spent shells, tossed them out the window, slipped in two new ones and clicked the gun shut again. She did it all with most professional skill.

"But if he was trying to sneak up on us, why did he laugh like that?"

From the doorway of the room Otto's voice said, "That was Richard. That's the noise he makes when someone scares him. But he never made it at night before."

"No," said Mrs. Fitzpatrick, "but no one ever climbed into his tree at night before. I knew there was something wrong the minute I heard him."

"Did you hit the man when you shot?" Otto asked hopefully.

"No," said Mrs. Fitzpatrick. "I didn't try to hit him. But I wanted him to know that we are prepared, and that he must stay away."

"I think," she went on, "from the fact that he was hiding in the tree, we can guess that he does not know Ellen is here. He was planning to hide and wait for daylight and watch."

"Do you think it was Mr. Gates?" Ellen asked.

"I think not. I think Mr. Gates went back to wherever it was he came from—to the man he calls 'the king'—and reported his failure. Having failed, I doubt that he would be sent to try again.

"But whoever he was, it's good luck for us that he gave himself away. For it lets us know two things: First, that they have not given up, and second, that they are still searching in this part of the forest. Those two things will help us decide what Ellen must do now."

"What must I do, then?" Ellen asked.

"That we will discuss in the morning. Right now both of you should try to go back to sleep. You will have a hard day tomorrow. And for the rest of the night I think we should all stay together in the living room."

Mrs. Fitzpatrick took the pillow and blanket from Ellen's bed and arranged them on the sofa. She made a pallet of blankets for Otto on the floor. She locked Ellen's room, both window and door; then she settled herself in the armchair with the gun close at hand.

"Go to sleep," she told the children. "I think there will be no more trouble tonight, and if there is, we are ready."

Ellen kept the handbag with the crown in it on the pillow by her head.

The Flight Up the Mountain

ELLEN slept in a jumpy sort of way. She woke up often, each time thinking she had heard a sound, and each time reassured when she saw a gray shadow in the dark room, Mrs. Fitzpatrick sitting in the big armchair with the loaded shotgun by her side. Otto never stirred on his pallet. Finally she must have fallen into a sounder sleep, because when she woke up again the black windows had turned gray with the light of early dawn, and Mrs. Fitzpatrick was shaking her gently by the shoulder.

Ellen sat up. Mrs. Fitzpatrick put a finger to her lips and beckoned her to follow. They walked silently, leaving Otto asleep, into Mrs. Fitzpatrick's bedroom. This was a room Ellen had not seen before, a large room with four windows, two looking out at the rising mountains, two into a flower garden, all misty in the early light. On one wall hung two paintings in matching frames, done in dark, somber oils. Both were portraits, one the face of a young man with a high forehead and fine features which, when you looked at them, changed from elegance to arrogance and back to elegance again.

The other was of a beautiful, fine-complexioned young woman with shadowy gray eyes and shining black hair. Ellen looked at it, then looked again with bewilderment because it was of someone she knew. But who? Then she looked at the eyes, which had not changed at all in half a century or so.

"It's you," she said to Mrs. Fitzpatrick.

"It was. A long time ago."

"But it's so beautiful," Ellen said. Mrs. Fitzpatrick smiled.

"The artist who painted it thought so; but artists, of course, can make their own beauty. At any rate he would never sell it, nor part with it as long as he lived. When he died, he left it to me."

She sat down on the edge of her bed and motioned toward a chair next to it.

"Sit down, Ellen. I have some serious things to tell you. Some of them I do not want Otto to hear, which is why I left him sleeping in the other room."

Ellen sat down. She said, "You mean about the man in the tree?"

"Partly that. But mainly this: I have decided what I think is best for you to do. If the intruder was looking for you, as I believe he was, he will not be made any less curious by the reception he got. He will decide that you probably are here, and he will be back, perhaps with friends. Therefore I think it is no longer safe for you here, and you must go."

"But go where?" said Ellen.

"Not back down to the highway. That will be watched, you may be sure. No, there is another road I can show you, an old logging road, partly overgrown now but still passable, that leads back straight over the mountains.

"You see, Mr. Gates was not taking you toward Lexington, nor even toward Kentucky. True, he started out in that direction, and you are now not so very far from Kentucky. But the road you were taking, the one where you saw the truck, leads south, away from Lexington. What his true destination was I do not know, but it was not Lexington.

"The highway to Lexington runs west, making a great curve around these mountains. But if you follow the logging road, you will rejoin it, and when you do you will not have too much farther to go."

"But can I walk that far?" asked Ellen. "How long will it take?"

"You can walk that far if you go slowly, steadily, rest often, and take supplies with you. The swelling in your ankle is almost gone. I have the supplies ready. With luck and care, you should reach the highway in three days—four at the most. It will be hard, but you can do it. I want you to take Otto with you."

"Take Otto!" said Ellen in amazement. "But why?"

"For two reasons. First, because he will help you. He is strong and smart and brave; he knows how to get along in the woods—he lives in them—and he will not lose the way. In any case, an expedition of two is always better than one. If one gets into difficulty, the other can help.

"The other reason is this: Otto is in trouble, a kind of

trouble that I cannot solve. I think that you and your Aunt Sarah can help him, if you will."

"But what kind of trouble?" Ellen asked, and then she thought a moment. "You mean—about the trucks?"

"There is much more than you realize. First, you must know that I am not his mother, nor do I know who his parents are. I found him more than six years ago, wandering, lost, hungry, crying, on the road that leads to this house. I took him in. He was perhaps two and a half, possibly three years old. He could speak only a few words. He knew his first name, but not his last. He had been abandoned on the highway, and if I had not found him, he would surely have died. He was half dead already, poor little baby."

"But he calls you his mother."

"He thinks I am his mother. Or rather, put it this way: he insists on thinking I am his mother. I tried to tell him the truth when he grew old enough to understand, but he refused to believe. He grew so dreadfully upset I have not dared to raise the question again. Deep down, I am sure he knows the truth, but he will not allow it to enter his thoughts. Because he needs a mother so terribly.

"And out of that need he has built a dream, partly true, partly good, but partly dangerous. In this dream I am old —that much is true—but I am also penniless, helpless, and wholly dependent on him. And that is not true, but to prove that it is, he goes to great lengths."

"That's why he steals things from the truck accidents," Ellen said.

"Things I do not need at all," Mrs. Fitzpatrick agreed. "But there is more to it than you know. The first of the wrecks was an accident; perhaps even the second. But the others were not.

"I learned this with certainty only recently—after the wreck you saw yourself, in fact. Yet I had been puzzled for some time, and worried. There had been too many trucks running off the road. Why? Finally I went and looked.

"I found, down the road, a sign warning of the curve ahead, warning cars and trucks to slow down. Near it, hidden in the woods, I found several large, leafy branches that had been cut loose—obviously with a hunting knife. And under the sign I found leaves from those branches.

"Otto has been going down to the highway at night and placing the branches in front of the sign so that drivers cannot see it. Ordinary cars can apparently make this curve even so without going off the road, but for heavy trucks it is too sharp. By good fortune, and only by good fortune, no one has been killed or injured—so far. But you can see why I feel Otto should leave."

Ellen was shocked. "That's terrible. But couldn't you tell him to stop?"

"I could, and he would obey. But then he would surely think of something else. No, the real solution is to get him away, let him live with younger, stronger people, and forget this strange dream he has built up."

"Well," Ellen said, "I would like him to come. But I don't know what Aunt Sarah will say."

"If she feels she must, she can bring him back. I will always take him in and do the best I can for him. I have grown to love him as if he were my own son, and I will miss him. And if she does bring him back, you will at least have had a companion on your trip. But I think she will not."

So it was decided, and Otto and Ellen, early that morning, got ready for their long walk. Mrs. Fitzpatrick did not tell Otto that he might be leaving forever, but only that he was to go with Ellen until she found her aunt.

The night before, she had sewed for Ellen a pair of sturdy slacks out of some heavy, denim-like material, much better for hiking than her wrinkled dress. She had also found somewhere a blouse and a light blue sweater, which was slightly big for Ellen but fit well enough if she turned the sleeves up at the wrists. And for both Ellen and Otto she had made a pair of cleverly designed bags like rucksacks that they could carry on their backs. Otto was delighted with his and put it on immediately. He had always wanted a knapsack.

They had a brown blanket apiece, for they would have to sleep in the woods and the nights were cool up in the mountains. There was food to fill the rucksacks: a special kind of biscuit Mrs. Fitzpatrick had made; it was tough, but tasted good, was nourishing, and would not, Mrs. Fitzpatrick said, go stale. They took dried apricots and raisins, some small jars of jam, some dried beef, a pot to cook it in and tin plates, and forks to eat with. They took bacon, which Otto knew how to cook on a stick, a dozen hard-boiled eggs, matches to light fires with, and a cake of soap to wash their hands and faces when they came to a brook. Otto put a metal water bottle, full, into his rucksack; they would refill it from streams along the way. His hunting knife, in a leather sheath, was strapped to his belt.

Ellen put her handbag containing the crown into her rucksack.

They were ready to go. Ellen actually felt rather gay, as if they were starting on a picnic, and Otto was jumping with excitement.

Mrs. Fitzpatrick walked with them for the first mile, to show them where the road was, though Otto was sure he already knew which road she meant. As they walked she told Ellen:

"When you get over the mountains and come down on the highway, turn left to go to Lexington. I think you should not try to hitchhike, but walk along the road until you come to a house that looks as if it might have a telephone in it—that is, any good-sized house. By this time you will be only a few hours by car from Lexington. Ask the people in the house if they will telephone to your Aunt Sarah, and when they do, talk to her and ask her to come and get you. If they have no phone, or refuse to help, just go on and try the next house.

"Be careful of the crown, whatever you do. It is priceless, and it has great powers for good. If you meet strangers who are unfriendly or even suspicious, or if you come to any situation that you are unsure of, try to hide it. Bury it in the woods if you must, in a place you can find again. But do not let it be taken from you. Whoever is looking for you is looking for the crown: they may not be sure you have it, since it might have been destroyed in the fire. But they are taking no chances. Especially, beware of any person, or group of people, who use the name *Hieronymus.*"

"Hieronymus?" repeated Ellen curiously. "Who is that?"

"The first Hieronymus was a saint, a holy man who lived more than a thousand years ago. He was a mystic and a great scholar, a student of religion. Over the centuries he has had many followers, some of whom also have used the name Hieronymus. Most of these were also religious men, but others formed groups who lived apart, often in caves, and studied strange and mysterious things that had nothing to do with religion, but with forces that are, I think, better left unstudied and unknown. It was one of these men who first wrote about a crown like yours. Whether he made it, or found it already made, I do not know. He made—or found—other devices, too. He was not a good man, nor were his followers.

"But many years ago—in fact, long before I was born —all of these things disappeared, and have been known about since only as legends, strange tales from manuscripts of the Dark Ages. And the cults of Hieronymus died out. Now the crown has reappeared, and there may be—though I have no knowledge of this—a new Hieronymus looking for it."

Otto, whose attention-span was considerably shorter than Ellen's, had lost interest in the cults of Hieronymus and run on ahead. Now he gave a whoop of joy.

"Look," he shouted. "Richard's coming with us." And sure enough, the crow fluttered out of the sky and settled on his shoulder.

"Can he come?" Ellen asked.

"Why not, if he will? He has already saved you once. Perhaps he will again."

They walked a little farther, and then Mrs. Fitzpatrick asked:

"Tell me. When you put the crown on your head, does it make you feel . . . different?" It was the first time Ellen had heard her hesitate.

Ellen thought a minute and then said, "Yes." Until now she had not realized it. "It does. It makes me feel . . ." Feel how? Stronger? Not exactly. Surer? That was closer. "It makes me feel surer of things. I don't know how. But it helps me to think." And it had, she knew now. It was because she had worn it even those few minutes, before the fire, that she had been able to think and go on after the disaster struck.

"I think that the more you wear it," Mrs. Fitzpatrick said, "the more different it will make you feel. And you will be better for it. The crown is, by itself, only a shiny toy. It is in combination with things—with you, and perhaps with other things—that it has power. I cannot explain it more clearly than that, because I do not understand it myself."

Now they reached the logging road, where Otto and Richard waited impatiently. It was one of those dirt roads with grass in the middle, but with two clear tracks where the earth has been packed hard by the wheels of innumerable trucks and wagons. Where they stood, this road cut through a clearing, a small field; then it disappeared from sight into the trees on its way up the mountain. By the height of the grass between the tracks it was clear that it was no longer used much, if at all.

"This is as far as I will go," Mrs. Fitzpatrick said. "Otto, come and kiss me goodbye." And he did, though in a most embarrassed way. "Ellen, I wish you safety, and remember what to tell your Aunt Sarah." She meant about

Otto, and Ellen understood.

Mrs. Fitzpatrick stood and watched a long time after they started up the road. The last time Ellen turned back she was wiping her eyes with a handkerchief, and then she set out for home, walking rather wearily. The two children strode up the trail in good cheer.

Otto the Knife

THEY make you look like a boy," Otto said. He was not paying a compliment, but just making an observation.

"What does?" Ellen said.

"The pants. And the shirt."

"Girls wear slacks all the time. You're old-fashioned."

"That's not what I meant. I meant in case somebody was watching."

"Watching what?"

"Watching us. When we left the house. They were looking for a girl. If they thought you were a boy, they'd give up."

"That's true," Ellen said. "I hadn't thought of it."

"Except your hair looks like a girl's hair. You should wear a hat."

"I don't have a hat."

"I know."

They were walking steadily along the two tracks of the

road, Ellen on the left, Otto on the right. They had come perhaps two miles since leaving Mrs. Fitzpatrick. The morning was still cool, birds sang over their heads, and their spirits were high. Here the road led through oak trees, choosing its way carefully where the great trunks were far enough apart for it to pass. It was taking them slowly upward toward a pass between two high mountains, so that on either side the ground and the forest sloped above them as far as they could see. A small brook had picked almost the same path, bubbling along parallel to the road, sometimes leaving it for a while, sometimes flowing right across it, so that they had to leap the water, or pick their way carefully on mossy green stepping stones.

"We could cut it off," Otto said thoughtfully.

"Cut what off?"

"Your hair."

"We don't have any scissors."

"I could do it with my knife." He pulled the knife from its sheath, as if he planned to start then and there. The idea of Otto's hacking at her hair with a knife did not appeal to Ellen at all.

"You could *not*," she said, a bit tartly. "Anyway, we're already out of sight, so it's too late."

"You don't need to get snotty about it."

"I'm not. And don't say *snotty*."

"Why not?"

"It's a vulgar word."

When Otto faced a dead end, he changed course.

"See that spot?" he said. He pointed with his knife at a circular scar on a tree trunk about fifteen feet ahead, where a limb had fallen off.

"Yes. The round one?"

Otto drew his arm back, the knife blade flashed through the sunlight, and the point buried itself deep in the very middle of the round spot, like an arrow in a bullseye. He did this so quickly Ellen's eye could hardly follow it.

"How did you do that?" she asked in astonishment.

"It's easy," Otto said. "I can do it every time." He ran to the tree and pulled the blade out. "See that skinny tree over there?" He pointed to a sapling perhaps two inches in diameter. Again his arm moved in an incredibly deft motion, and the blade was in the sapling, humming softly.

"Let me try," Ellen said.

"You won't be able to. It takes practice."

He was right. When Ellen threw the knife it struck handle-to and clattered uselessly to the ground. She tried again, with the same result. She gave it back to Otto.

"Do it slower," she said, "so I can see how."

"I can't. When I do it slower, I can't do it."

"How did you learn?"

"I read in a book about a Chinese murderer who killed people by throwing knives at them. It was neat. No *bang* or anything; the people just fell down dead, and the Chinaman always got away before anybody knew what happened."

"His fingerprints would be on the knife."

"He wore gloves. Anyway, I drew a picture of a Chinaman on a plank and tried throwing a pocketknife at it. Pocketknives are no good, though. The handle's too heavy."

"But how could the Chinaman in the story get his knife back?"

"He didn't. He just left it in their hearts and got another one. He had boxes of them. Then I practiced with an ice-pick. That worked better, only it was too light. It wouldn't go very far. Then I got this knife. I practiced for months, almost every day."

"It's sort of dangerous."

"No it's not. I mean, I'm not going to throw it *at* anybody."

"You'd hurt them if you did."

"Hurt them?" Otto said scornfully. "They'd drop dead."

They kept walking as they talked, and in another mile or so the trail leveled off: they had reached the top of the first pass. But ahead they could see much higher mountains rising, some with rocky shoulders too steep for trees to grow on. From where they stood they could not see how or where the road crossed these, but it was leading straight toward them, so it was clear that they had a climb ahead. Still, if wagons had made it, so could they.

Richard stayed with them, sometimes riding on Otto's shoulder, sometimes flashing from branch to branch above them like a blue-black shadow. Every now and then he vanished entirely for three or four minutes, flying a scouting expedition, ahead or back or off through the woods to one side. When he returned to Otto's shoulder after one of these, he always squawked quietly, as if to say, "I'm back."

Along the way Ellen found a blackberry bush growing beside the road and lagged behind Otto for a few seconds to pick a handful of berries. As she set out again, she felt a rustle of wind on her cheek, heard a small voice say,

"Eat," and Richard, back from a mission, had settled on her shoulder. She held out a berry, and the black bill tweaked it gently from between her thumb and finger.

She called to Otto in delight, "Look at Richard."

Otto obviously felt quite proud of Richard.

"He likes you," he said. "That's the first time he ever sat on anybody's shoulder besides mine."

As for Richard, he was interested primarily in the blackberries. He gripped Ellen's shoulder gently, his talons tickling slightly, his soft wing-feathers brushing her cheek, until he had eaten all the berries she had. Then he flew back to the bush to pick some more of his own. But from then on, he was as likely to settle on Ellen's shoulder as on Otto's; she got used to feeling the puff of air and the sudden light weight.

The sun rose higher and beamed through the trees with steady intensity; even in the mountains it grows hot at midday in summer. Ellen took off her sweater. She found herself seeking out the shady side of the road—when there was a shady side—and felt her blouse grow wet with sweat under the rucksack. Small clouds of gnats hummed around their heads and got in their hair, ears, eyes and noses. With Otto's knife they cut switches of leaves to fan them away, which helped a little but not much. Then the level stretch of road ended. Just ahead it began rising steeply, and the oak forest became mixed with pine. Off the road to the left the brook ran through a shady grove.

"It's lunch time," Otto decreed.

"How can you tell?" Ellen said, not that she disagreed. But neither of them had a watch.

"The sun's straight up, so it must be noon. Anyway, my

belly knows." He patted his stomach.

"That's a vulgar word, too," Ellen said.

They walked over to the brook, unloaded their rucksacks gratefully, and sat down. Their legs were tired, and
Ellen rubbed her ankle, which, strangely, had not hurt at
all while she was walking on it, but started to now, though
only a little.

They selected food from their stores: biscuits and rasp-
berry jam and a couple of hardboiled eggs sprinkled with
salt; they drank fresh cold water from the brook, remembering to refill the water bottle. Since they had hiked hard
all morning, everything tasted delicious.

After lunch they lay on their backs and looked at the
sky through the trees.

"What's your Aunt Sarah like?" asked Otto. "Old or
young?"

"Young. She's not even married yet."

"That doesn't prove she's young. She might be an old
maid."

"She is *not*," Ellen said. "She'll get married when she
gets older."

"Who to?"

"How do I know? But I know she will. She's pretty—
she's beautiful."

"Is she rich?"

"I don't know. I guess so. She has a big house, and two
maids and a gardener."

"When I grow up I'm going to have millions of dollars.
Then I'll build a big store, an enormous store, right near
my mother's house. It'll have everything in it: food,
clothes, dogs, guns, firewood, cars, beds, and cokes."

"A department store," Ellen said. "But they don't have cars in department stores."

"This one will. And everybody who buys anything will have to pay, so I'll make even more money, except my mother. When she wants anything, she can just walk over to the store and pick it out. When they try to make her pay, she'll have a special card that says she can have it free."

"Like a charge plate," Ellen said.

"What's a charge plate?"

"It's like what you said. You go to the store and buy something, and when it's time to pay you give them a card with your name on it and say, 'Charge it.' But they send you a bill later, so you have to pay anyway."

"They won't send my mother any bill. I'll tell them not to. It's my store."

"I wish I had a card like that," Ellen said, thinking of all the big stores she had been in and all the things in them.

"Okay, you can have one, too. And I'll have one. But nobody else. Otherwise I'll lose money."

"Thank you," Ellen said. It did sound like a nice idea. But she remembered what Mrs. Fitzpatrick had told her about Otto. Still, it was a generous sort of dream.

They repacked their things, shouldered their rucksacks and went on. They were refreshed by the lunch and the short rest; even so they set out at a considerably slower pace than they had in the morning. The trip no longer seemed so much like a picnic, but rather more like a forced march. Even Richard was less inclined to swoop about. He was content to ride, looking rather drowsy, on one or the other of their shoulders.

As the road rose higher, the oak trees disappeared behind them, and they walked through a deep, dark green pine forest. This was a stiller kind of woods, with fewer birds; the pine needles muffled the sound of their footsteps, and they walked in silence. The road turned rocky underfoot, and more and more frequently they saw great gray stone outcroppings, and steep rock cliffs where nothing grew at all.

At length they came to a place where a huge pine tree, uprooted by the wind, had fallen across the road. Although it had long been dead, its spiny branches formed an impenetrable barrier, and they had to detour around it.

Otto said, "That proves nobody goes over this road anymore. They would have cut the tree away." And yet, a minute later, curiously, he found he was wrong, for when they walked into the woods to go around the tree they could see there was a definite path already there.

"Maybe animals made it," Ellen said. "It might be a deer track."

But Otto, who knew quite a lot about tracks, found, in a place where the pine needles had been scuffed away, a curved indentation.

"That's from a man's shoe," he said. "A heel mark. I know it is." And Ellen, when she looked closely, could see that it did look like one. A little farther along the path Otto found another bare spot where there were several more of the tracks, all the same size, as if they were made by the same shoes, some curving in one direction, some in the opposite.

"Somebody walks back and forth through here," Otto

said. "But not very often, or there'd be more tracks. You can hardly see some of them—they're old."

And this was puzzling, because since leaving Mrs. Fitzpatrick early that morning they had seen no sign of a house, nor any human being.

Now the road changed again, and to Ellen's mind at least, changed much for the worse. Where it had been following a high valley, so that the ground rose on either side, it now deserted the valley and clung directly to the mountainside, following a natural ledge, or shelf, cut out of a very steep, very high slope. In fact, in places it was not a slope at all; a rock cliff rose sheer as a wall on their left, and fell straight down on their right. It was the straight down that Ellen didn't like. It made her dizzy to think about it, much less look down it, and she walked as close to the left side of the road as she could, picking her way carefully so she would not stumble, since the road was narrow here, and there were loose rocks lying all over it.

Otto was not bothered in the least; he strode fearlessly along the edge and occasionally—when the drop-off was particularly steep—picked up a large stone and tossed it over the edge. Then they would listen, and sometimes it seemed as if a whole minute went by before they heard the *clunk* as the stone crashed on other stones far below.

Ellen did not much like this game, but what really worried her was this: if the road continued this way until dark, they would have to stop walking for fear of stepping over the ledge—and then where would they sleep? The ground underfoot was nothing but hard, sharp rocks, and anyway, who could sleep when just turning over might send you flying down a cliff?

So she watched uneasily while the sun turned from white to orange and then red as it sank in the evening sky, and as the great shadows of the mountains crept like black clouds over the forest in the valley below. She walked grimly on, and made Otto keep walking, too, although both their legs were tired now, and their feet felt like cinder blocks.

At last, as they came around a curve in the mountain side, Ellen thought she saw, far ahead, a glimmer of green near the road. Another half mile and she was sure of it: they were coming to the top of this particular shoulder of the mountain; the steep slope flattened out, and there was forest again. They staggered the last few hundred yards in silence, turned without a word off the rocky road into the pines, and fell exhausted onto the brown carpet of needles.

But after a few minutes of resting Otto's energy began to return. He propped his head on one fist.

"I wonder how far we walked," he said.

"How can you tell?" Ellen said without moving. "There's no way to measure how far you walk."

"Yes there is. You measure how fast you walk—how many miles an hour—and then you figure out how long you've been walking, and then multiply."

"Sure, if you *know*. But we don't know how fast we walked, or how long, either."

"I bet we walked fifty miles."

"Not that far," Ellen said. "Soldiers can only march

thirty miles a day, even when they train every day. I read it in a book."

"We've got to make a fire," Otto said.

"Yes," Ellen said. "In a few minutes."

"But not here."

"Why not?"

"You can see it from the road. I mean in case somebody's following us. We've got to move farther back into the woods."

So they rested a little longer, and then walked another quarter-mile or so to a spot where, in the thick forest, their fire would be invisible. There was plenty of firewood lying about, for the pines around had shed their lower branches. Otto scraped away all the pine needles from a wide circle; pine needles burn fiercely and can set the woods afire. Then, using a handful of them as tinder, he got a blaze going, using only a single match to start it.

They put some of the dried beef in their cooking pot, added some potatoes, which Ellen peeled and sliced up with Otto's knife, and some water, and in a few minutes the clearing was filled with the warm smell of beef stew. They decided to ration their water this way: one-third for cooking, one-third for drinking, and one-third for tomorrow, since they could not be sure when they would come to another brook.

They ate the stew—all of it, even though they had cooked all the pot would hold—and sopped up the gravy with more biscuits. They had not enough water to wash the pot, but Ellen wiped it dry with a clump of green pine needles. Then they fixed their beds, Otto showing Ellen how to roll up in her blanket, first piling pine needles under one end of it to serve as a pillow. When darkness came, they slept. Ellen woke up once during the night: she heard someone moving, but it was only Otto, putting some more wood on the fire. Richard slept high in a pine tree.

King and Mr. Carver

WHEN Ellen awoke again, the sun was up; Richard was standing on her chest chuckling to himself; and she smelled breakfast. Otto had waked up hungry, had cut, peeled and pointed some thin branches of green pine, and skewered strips of bacon on them. The branches, one end stuck in the ground, leaned over the coals of the fire; the bacon sizzled and dropped bits of melted fat. Each drop made a little burst of flame when it landed, and even the smoke smelled edible.

"I'm stiff," Ellen said. Richard clucked in surprise and bounced into the air.

"So was I," Otto said. "It goes away when you walk around."

Ellen sat up, then stood, trying her legs. They felt as if they were black and blue all over, only on the inside instead of the outside.

"Walk over to the road and back," Otto said. "You'll

see." He was busy with breakfast.

Ellen tried it, and as usual he was right. By the time she came back to the fire, the stiffness was mostly gone except for her ankle, and even that was not very sore. She looked to see if it was swollen. It was not.

"Here's your breakfast." Otto handed her a tin plate. He had split some biscuits, toasted them lightly on the coals, placed strips of bacon between the halves and put them back together. Bacon sandwiches, and beside them a hard-boiled egg, all peeled. Otto obviously woke up feeling energetic and efficient.

They ate quickly, drank a little water, wiped the plates, covered the fire with dirt, shouldered their rucksacks and were on their way. Once back on the trail, they found it continued through the woods, for the time being at least, and as if to make up for the ordeal of yesterday afternoon, stayed nearly level most of the time and even went slightly downhill for a couple of miles. At the bottom of the downhill part they found a wide, shallow brook flowing across the road on a bed of solid rock. They had to take off their shoes and socks to wade across; the water was ice cold, but only ankle-deep. Here they were able to wash their plates, their cooking pot, and their hands and faces. Then they rinsed the water bottle and refilled it.

It was a mile or so beyond this brook, heading uphill again, that Richard began behaving in a strange and alarming manner. Coming back from one of his regular exploring flights, he did not land on either of their shoulders as usual, but instead flew high into the air, straight over their heads. There he emitted a series of loud, piercing *"caws,"* which echoed up and down the valley. Then he plummeted like a hawk to a tree by the roadside, where he sat, high up, beating his wings angrily. In a few seconds he took off again, heading back in the direction from which they had come—toward the brook—cawing steadily.

"Someone is coming," Otto said.

"How do you know?"

"Because that's what he does when he sees somebody."

"Where?"

"Can't tell. I guess down the road where we came."

"Who could it be?"

"I'll tell you one thing," Otto said. "Whoever it is, it's a stranger."

"A stranger?"

"Ever since we saw those footprints by the pine tree, I've been watching for tracks. I haven't seen any. Tracks don't show much in a hard road like this, I know. But if people came up here, there'd be some sign, and there isn't."

"Oh," Ellen said. "I see. Do you think . . . ?"

"It's someone chasing us? It might be."

"What should we do?"

"Hide. And watch. And don't leave any signs, because whoever it is may be watching, too."

They looked around. Off to their right, up the hillside, there was a thick grove of trees with a clump of bushes growing in front of them. Leading up to it was a gully, a sort of ravine with stones in the bottom—no doubt a stream bed in the spring, when snows were melting down the mountains, but dry now. In any case, the stones would show no footprints.

"Up there," Otto said, and in a moment they were stumbling up the steep bank over the sliding stones. They reached the grove, puffing hard, and put down their rucksacks. They discovered that if they crouched down, rather uncomfortably, they could watch the road through the bushes without being seen.

"Now," Otto whispered, "stay quiet." They were perhaps sixty feet from the road, looking down on it. Their panting subsided in a minute, and they breathed very softly, not daring to move. They had no way of knowing how far behind them the stranger—if indeed there was a stranger—would be walking, nor how fast.

After what seemed to Ellen like an hour, Otto whispered:

"I hear him. He's coming."

His ears must have been keener than hers, for she heard nothing. But then, in a few seconds, they both saw the dark figure of a man emerge from the woods far down the road. He was a stranger, true enough, and a strange and frightening sight. He was tall and lean and completely dressed in black: black hat, black coat of an odd cut that looked like a cape, black pants, and black boots—but there was a single streak of color: up the side of each boot ran a slash of green, a shiny green that Ellen had seen before. His face was dark, somber, and gaunt, the face of an angry mortician, a grim hunter.

He was walking swiftly, purposefully, and at every pace his sharp, black eyes looked piercingly to the left, to the right, ahead, downward, upward; then again, left, right, ahead, down, up. He was not walking for pleasure, nor for destination. He was searching.

Just watching him come up the road threw a cold terror into both their hearts. They froze stock still, and could not have moved if they had wanted to. They waited, scarcely breathing, for him to pass and disappear. And then, just as he was directly in front of them, it happened.

There was a sudden, noisy shaking, rustling, rattling of limbs and leaves in a tree directly overhead, scarcely six feet above them. They did not dare move, even enough to look up. But they knew what it was: Richard had chosen this moment to flutter from one branch to another in a most clumsy way.

The stranger stopped in his tracks and turned. Obviously he had heard the noise, but could not tell what or quite where it was. Now he looked straight toward them. Ellen's heart stopped; she was sure his eyes could pierce the bushes and see her face. He reached toward his coat pocket—for a gun?

Then Richard moved again, higher, and the eyes shifted and looked above them. The man stopped suddenly, picked up a stone and threw it, hard, at the tree where the noise was coming from. It crashed through the branches and out the other side, missing Richard but sending him flapping out of the tree toward the sky, cawing furiously as he flew.

The stranger watched him fly off. Then he stood a moment, scrutinizing the tree and the bushes. He took a tentative step toward them. Ellen held her breath and got ready to run. Then he stopped; you could almost hear him thinking: "Why bother? It was only a crow." He had, after all, passed dozens of them during the day. To their intense relief, he turned and went on down the road, still walking swiftly, still looking, looking, looking in all directions.

"Whew," Otto said, after the stranger was safely out of sight, "That's the scariest-looking man I ever saw."

"He was looking for us," Ellen said. "I know it."

"I guess he was. He was certainly looking for something."

"I wonder what we should do now."

"I think we should wait here a while, until he gets way ahead of us. Then we could go on."

"But suppose he turns around and comes back?"

"We'll have to keep watching. Richard will probably spot him."

"But suppose he doesn't? Suppose the man decides to hide in the trees the way we did? And watch for us? Or suppose he sneaks up on us at night?"

"But he thinks we're ahead of him."

"He thinks so now. But he's going so fast, after a while he's going to decide that we must be behind him."

"Or that we didn't come this way at all," Otto said optimistically.

But Ellen felt that in a situation like this you had to plan for the worst rather than hope for the best.

"He won't do that," she said.

They moved from their uncomfortable crouch behind the bushes and walked back into the trees. Ellen was worried. Perhaps, she thought, the best thing to do would be to wait here, keeping watch, until the stranger did come back. Then if he kept walking in the opposite direction, they could safely go on. But this wait might delay them for hours—possibly even days.

While she was thinking, Otto made a discovery.

"Look," he said. "Here's a path."

Leading from the end of the stony gully they had climbed to get up the hill, there was a faint but clearly perceptible trail. It curved on up the hill and then around behind the bushes where they had been hiding, through the trees where they now stood. As it curved, it gradually turned parallel to the road and disappeared into the shadowy woods ahead of them.

This, Ellen realized, might be the answer to their problems. For if they could walk along this path, they would be going the same way the road went—keeping it in sight so they could see if the stranger returned, and keeping themselves out of sight. If only it continued in this direction.

Otto, like a hound on a trail, had his face practically to the ground.

"You know what?" he said. "These tracks are made by the same shoes we saw before, near that pine tree. At least they look the same. And the newest footprints are a couple of weeks old, maybe more. So whoever it was, he's not around here now. He's gone on long before."

They shouldered their rucksacks again and walked down the path, rather cautiously, to see where it led. To Ellen's delight, after half a mile or more it was still running alongside the road, perhaps a hundred feet to the right of it and above it. Now and then, where the trees were too thick, they lost sight of it, but it always reappeared after a few paces.

Because they were watching the road instead of looking ahead, they were taken by surprise. There was a sound directly in front of them. Ellen turned and gasped. Not ten feet away, in the middle of the trail, stood the biggest, fiercest-looking dog she had ever seen.

It was a mastiff, gigantic, heavy-shouldered, with a huge head and jaws like a lion's. Its teeth were bared, and from its chest came a deep, rumbling growl.

Otto, in an act of sheer bravery, leaped instantly in front of Ellen. As he leaped his hand flashed and the knife was in it. For a moment they stood there, the great dog bristling, poised to charge, the small boy motionless, eyes bright and alert, his gleaming knife balanced and ready.

Then a man's calm voice said, "Down, King, down. Can't you see it's just a couple of kids?"

Up the hill a few feet, leaning against a tree, stood a tall, pleasant-looking man. His hair was brown, his clothes were brown, and he puffed on a brown briar pipe.

He said, "And now, boy, if you'll put away that knife, we can talk. Don't worry. King won't hurt anyone unless I tell him to."

Otto put the knife back in its sheath, and the man walked down the hill. He shook hands with both of them.

"My name is Jason Carver," he said. "Come on in and rest a while. Since you're here, I know you must have walked a long way."

Now they saw where the trail had been leading. Straight ahead stood two cabins, almost invisible in the pine woods because they were made of rough pine logs.

A White Dove

MR. CARVER led them into the nearest of the cabins. "First we will have some lunch. You must be hungry."

Ellen argued politely, but not very hard, "Thank you very much, but we brought our own food with us. It's in the knapsacks."

"Of course you did," said Mr. Carver cheerfully, "but when you visit me, you eat my food. That's the rule of the house. Besides, I have two big trout I caught just this morning."

He put the trout in a black skillet, each one almost a foot long and still damp from the stream, and put the skillet on the stove, and in a minute the fresh trout smell filled the room and wafted out the open window. Ellen was glad, for she welcomed a change from bread and hard-boiled eggs, which is what they would have had for lunch.

She looked around the inside of the cabin. It was big, roughly built, and quite bare, but clean and comfortable enough. There was a cot, a pine table, a few straight chairs, a big bookcase full of books, a wooden chest, and that was about all except for the stove and a rather drab deerskin rug, on which King had settled himself with a loud thump and gone to sleep.

Then she saw something else. In one corner, on a small shelf, stood two of the most beautiful woodcarvings she had ever seen.

Both were women's heads, life-sized, intricately cut from some light reddish wood polished to a gentle glow. Ellen walked over and stared at them. One face was older, one younger, but otherwise they looked alike. Even the brows and eyelashes looked real, each hair finely etched with a sharp tool.

"You like my statues," said Mr. Carver.

"Oh, *yes,*" Ellen said. "Where did you get them?"

"I carved them. I'm a sculptor. At least, that's how I make my living."

"But . . ." Ellen began, and then hesitated.

"But why am I living alone, way up here in the mountains?"

"Well, yes," Ellen said. "I did wonder."

"I like it up here," said Mr. Carver. "I like the woods, and the quiet, and the stream that flows down the mountain. I can work in peace, and read and think. It's true, there's more to it than that, but it can keep until later.

"Anyway, I think I should have the right to ask first: what are two children doing alone, way up here in the mountains? After all, it was you who came walking into my front yard."

"I'm sorry," Ellen said. "We didn't know . . ."

"Of course you didn't," said Mr. Carver, smiling. "Anyway, I'm glad of the company. Still, it isn't every day that visitors get this far, so naturally I'm curious."

"It's because there was a man chasing us," Otto said. "At least we think he was chasing us, so we hid in the woods. Then we found the path—your path."

"A man chasing you. Are you runaways, then?"

"Oh, no," said Ellen. "We're going to visit my aunt."

"I see," said Mr. Carver dubiously.

'Well, we're running away from *him*," Otto said. "But so would anyone. He's dangerous."

"Who is he?" asked Mr. Carver. "What does he look like?"

They described the stranger, emphasizing that he was dressed all in black except for the green stripes on his boots. They told how he had come hurrying up the road, obviously looking for someone or something.

"Very odd," said Mr. Carver. "He's certainly nobody I know. I wonder what he *is* looking for."

"For us," said Ellen. "I'm sure of it."

"But what would he want with you?"

They gave him a garbled account of the events of the past few days. Garbled partly because they were both telling it at once, partly because they had had to leave parts of it out: they did not want to tell about the crown, for instance, and Ellen felt she should not tell about the wrecked trucks, nor Otto's troubles.

Mr. Carver seemed skeptical. "Someone climbed a tree outside your house," he said. "What makes you think there's any connection between that and this man in black? And how can you say he's dangerous? He threw a stone at a crow—farmers do that every day. He didn't know it was your crow. How do you know he's not just a hunter, looking for deer, maybe?"

Ellen and Otto were dismayed. They were so *sure,* and yet, of course, Mr. Carver was right—they couldn't prove it at all; they had no way of really knowing who the stranger was.

Mr. Carver changed the subject.

"Let's talk about it after lunch," he said. "The trout are ready and so are we."

So he cut up the fish and served it on three plates, along with some small new potatoes from his garden, which had been boiling in a pot on the stove, and some sweet butter.

Mr. Carver poured himself a cup of coffee from a gray coffeepot, and said, "When we're through, would you like to see my workshop and some of the things I've made? It's in the other cabin."

"I would," said Ellen.

"Okay," said Otto, obviously not very interested in art.

So in a few minutes Mr. Carver and King led the way to the other cabin, which was identical in size and shape to the one he lived in, but had more and bigger windows.

He opened the door and they stepped into a sunlit room that seemed like a fairy tale. The walls, where there were not windows, were covered with shelves, and the shelves with carvings, large and small, polished to a soft, translucent glow. There were statues of prancing horses, of leaping deer; there was a Madonna with a plaintive face, a sleeping panther of some jet-black wood, and a dove of pearl white. And there were faces, faces, faces, some ugly, some beautiful, nearly all sad. There were several more, Ellen noticed, all on one shelf, of the same woman and girl she had seen in the other cabin. One of these, of the girl, was smiling, but even so she looked sad.

Ellen was completely delighted; she walked from shelf to shelf, staring. She wanted to pick up the white dove, which was no bigger than her hand and had a sweet expression on its face, but she did not dare. So Mr. Carver picked it up and handed it to her.

"If you like the dove so much," he said, "you'd better keep it."

"Oh," Ellen said. "I couldn't."

"Of course you could. I've got another one."

"Where?" Ellen asked, for she had seen only one.

"Here," said Mr. Carver. He turned to a long table which stood against one wall. Behind it were arrayed rows of knives, chisels, files, hammers, tiny picks and awls of every size and shape; under it stood blocks on blocks of wood of many grains and colors. Mr. Carver picked out a white block about the size of a shoe box.

"There's a dove in here," he said. "You can't see him yet, but he's in there."

"Maybe not *just* like this one. You can't be sure of that until you cut away all the wood that's holding him in. His wings may be spread a little wider, or his head may be turned at a different angle. You see, he has something to say about that—almost as much as I do."

"Like Pinocchio," Ellen said.

"In a way," said Mr. Carver, "though none of my wood has ever talked to me. Not so far, at least."

Otto was getting interested in spite of himself.

"You mean you just take that hunk of wood and whittle, and make a bird like that?"

"That's right," said Mr. Carver. "But it's a very careful kind of whittling, and you have to have a pretty clear idea of what the bird looks like. Also, you have to learn how gently to tap a sharp chisel so that it doesn't cut too deep, and what shape of chisel or knife to use, and how hard different kinds of wood are, what color they will turn when you polish them, and which kinds will split and which won't, and a lot of other things."

"But how did you learn all that? Could I learn it?"

"You can if you're willing to work at it. As to how I learned it—that's pretty much like the question Ellen asked: why do I live up here alone in the mountains?"

In front of the work table there stood a tall wooden stool and a low bench. Mr. Carver sat down on the stool and picked up a block of wood and a small, sharp blade. The two children sat on the bench and watched and listened.

The Woodcarver's Story

AT least," Mr. Carver continued, "the answers to both questions can be told at once. As I said, I like living up here. I like to hunt and to fish, I don't like crowds of people, and I like to be independent. Here I can grow most of my own food in my garden. I have plenty of fish for the catching, and there's game in the woods.

"So I have little need for money—just to buy clothes now and then, books, a few tools, a sack of flour. When I need those, I pack up some of my carvings and walk down the same way you walked up. I go maybe four or five times a year."

"I knew it!" said Otto. "I saw your tracks along the way. Didn't I, Ellen?"

"Then you have a sharp eye," Mr. Carver said, "because it's been a month or more since I've been down. There's a town a few miles along the highway, and a store in it that buys my carvings. Apparently they have no trouble selling them, because they always buy all I have."

Then he added, "But getting back to the question. It's true I haven't always lived alone. I had a family once—a wife and a daughter, a little girl named Eliza.

"I was a stonecutter in those days. That is, I worked in a quarry, where we used big diamond-edged saws to cut blocks of granite. We sold these, some to make buildings, others to make pillars and statues and monuments, mostly gravestones.

"I became skilled at stonecutting, and so eventually I was promoted. I left the quarry and went to the factory, owned by the same company that made the monuments. In my spare time I studied stone sculpture, but at the factory I worked at making and carving gravestones.

"Then a terrible thing happened. In the middle of a bitter cold winter, the town where we lived had an epidemic of flu. Neither my wife nor my daughter was strong enough to resist it; both became dreadfully sick, and both of them died quite suddenly, on the same day. It was a sad time for me. I hardly knew what I was doing, so friends arranged for a funeral at a little church we used to go to. It was a busy place for funerals that winter.

"After the service was ended my friends and I walked through a snowstorm to the cemetery, and I watched my family buried in the frozen ground. When I saw the gravestones, a small one for Eliza, who was only eight, and a bigger one for my wife, I recognized them—for I had made them both myself just a few days earlier. Someone else at the factory had added only the names and dates.

"I realized then that I could never carve a stone again without thinking of that cold, sad day. I quit my job at the factory and moved away. For a long time after that I drifted from town to town, not knowing what to do with myself. Then I found a job in a cabinet-making shop—the same store that sells my woodcarvings.

"Though I could no longer carve in stone, I enjoyed working with wood. Stone is cold and hard and dead; wood is alive and warm. I tried doing wood sculpture and found to my surprise that people were eager to buy my work.

"But I also found that without my wife and daughter I felt lonelier when I was with other people than when I was alone. I began taking long walks in these mountains, and I felt happy here. So I bought these acres and built the two cabins—and here I am."

His sad story, though he told it matter-of-factly enough, had brought Ellen close to tears, and she did not know what to say next. But as he talked, Mr. Carver had been cutting away deftly at the block of wood he held; and now, with a smile, he handed it to Otto. It was his way of changing the subject.

Otto looked at it.

"It's me!" he said. He showed it to Ellen. Mr. Carver had made a hand-sized miniature of Otto's face, like him to the last eyelash. In the eyes he had captured the same alert, slightly wary expression; the mouth looked as if it were ready to speak.

"I *want* to learn how to do that," Otto said. "That's what I want to be when I grow up—a woodcarver."

"I thought you wanted to be a millionaire," Ellen said.

"I do," Otto said. "I'll be both."

"I wouldn't count on that," Mr. Carver said dryly.

"Anyway, it's not something you have to decide right now. If you want to learn woodcarving, there's no reason why you shouldn't try. Can you draw?"

"Yes," Otto said. "I'm good at drawing."

"That's the first step," said Mr. Carver. "Learning to draw, and learning to look at things carefully so that you see what they're really like. Woodcarving, or any kind of sculpture, for that matter, is really drawing, only you use a chisel or a blade or a file instead of a pen or a brush. And you work in three dimensions instead of two.

"Study drawing when you go back to school. Work hard at it, and in a few years, when you're good at it, get some woodworking tools. Then come back and see me and I'll show you how to use them."

"I'll do it," Otto said. "I really will. And I know the way here from my house now. If you don't move away again."

"I won't move away," Mr. Carver promised.

At this point the conversation was interrupted by two sounds: a series of alarmed, clarion caws from Richard outside the window, and a rumbling growl from King, who stood up, the hair along his spine rising like porcupine quills.

"We have a visitor," said Mr. Carver.

"Somebody's coming," said Ellen.

"It's him," cried Otto. "He's found us."

"We don't know who it is yet," said Mr. Carver. And he added, "Even if it is the same man, you have no real reason to think he's chasing you. But if it will make you feel better, you can stay hidden in here. I'll go outside and talk to whoever it is."

With that, Mr. Carver opened the door and called King,

who was still rumbling, to go with him. He stepped out of the cabin and shut the door behind him.

The two children crept back to the far side of the room and stood in the shadow of the work table. They could see and hear quite well through the open window; they hoped whoever was coming could not see equally well into the cabin.

The Stranger Returns

MR. CARVER said to King: "Stay," and pointed to the trunk of a big tree. King crouched under the tree and did not move. They could hear a noisy rattling of bushes along the path leading to the cabin; whoever was approaching was beating them as he came, the way a hunter flushes game.

Then the noise stopped. The visitor had seen the cabin itself. And in another minute he stood facing Mr. Carver outside the window. It was the stranger.

He wasted no words.

"Where are the children?" he said. His voice grated like a steel rasp. He did not pretend to be friendly.

"Who are you?" asked Mr. Carver. He did not sound particularly cordial, either.

"Where are the children?" the stranger repeated.

"What children?" said Mr. Carver.

"Don't play games," said the stranger. "I know they

came this way. I saw their tracks."

"What you saw and what you know are of no interest to me," said Mr. Carver coolly. 'If you would like to tell me who you are, and what you want and why, I will listen if you make it brief. Otherwise I have nothing to say to you but this: you are trespassing on my land. Get off, and get off now."

The stranger's hand snapped from beneath his coat, and the blue barrel of a pistol pointed at Mr. Carver's chest.

"Open the door of the cabin," he said. "I am going to find them and take them with me. If you try to stop me, I will kill you."

Mr. Carver did not move, but said two words:

"King: *guard!*"

There was a blurred streak of brown fur, and the stranger was on his back with two huge forepaws on his chest; the big jaws, teeth bared, were an inch from his throat. King was not growling now. He was absolutely silent. As the stranger went down, his gun clattered to the ground. It lay inches from his hand.

"I warn you," Mr. Carver said, "do not move a muscle. I have only to say one word, and you will never move again." And he walked over, picked up the gun, flicked it open, threw away the bullets, and tossed it in the cabin window.

"Now," said Mr. Carver, "the dog and I will escort you to the road. You will walk back down the mountain where you came from. Do not attempt to return. We can see the road from here, and the dog will be watching for you. He will not let you pass."

Mr. Carver snapped his fingers, and King came to heel. Without a word the stranger stood up, turned his back, and walked down the path, with the dog and Mr. Carver following.

Ellen sighed with relief.

"What a dog!" whispered Otto.

"That man nearly killed Mr. Carver," Ellen said.

"Yes, but we've got his gun now. Anyway, Mr. Carver wasn't scared a bit."

"Well, I was."

"I wasn't," Otto said, and Ellen saw that he had his knife in his hand. "He'd never have got through the door."

"I forgot about the knife," Ellen said. "Still, I'm glad he didn't try to come in. It would be awful if you had to throw it at somebody."

"Better than getting shot."

"I suppose so. But he wasn't going to shoot us. He said he was going to take us with him. I wonder where?"

"To their hideout."

"What hideout?"

"I think Mr. Gates and that stranger are gangsters. I bet there are others in with them, too. They want to kidnap you and take you to their hideout."

"But why?"

"Because they want the crown, that's why. It's probably worth a lot of money."

"Shh," Ellen said. "Mr. Carver's coming back."

"We can tell him about it."

"I guess we could. But why should we? There's no reason to."

Mr. Carver came into the cabin alone.

"I left King down by the road," he said, "to see your friend out of sight and make sure he keeps going in the right direction."

He picked up the gun from the floor of the cabin, aimed it out the window, clicked the trigger to make sure it was empty, and then laid it on a shelf.

"An ugly weapon," he said. "And an ugly man. But he certainly proved your story. He was looking for you—no doubt about that anymore. And from the way he acted, he meant you no good."

"Otto thinks he's trying to kidnap us."

"Probably for ransom," Otto lied quickly. "Her aunt's rich."

"That's possible," Mr. Carver admitted. "But still it's puzzling. How would he know about your aunt? How would he even know you have an aunt?"

"You forget," Ellen said, "I told Mr. Gates. We think they're working together."

"But you didn't tell Mr. Gates until after you were in his car. Why did he ask you to ride in the first place?"

"I don't know," Ellen said. "But they must have found out somehow."

"Maybe they hired a private eye," Otto said, "and he put a bug in your house. They do that all the time in detective stories."

"There's not much use in trying to guess," said Mr. Carver. "The point is, somebody really is trying to catch you. You need to get over the mountains and find your aunt, and then she will probably want to go to the police.

"King and I can't guard the road forever, but we can guard it for the next few days, and by that time you'll be there. But you should keep moving steadily and reasonably fast."

"How much farther is it before we reach the highway?" Ellen asked.

"I don't know exactly, because I've never been that way. But I think this cabin is about the halfway mark, and I know the road goes over one more high pass; higher, I've heard, than any you've come over so far."

"So we ought to be there in two more days," Ellen said.

"Yes, but to be safe, we'll watch the road for four." Mr. Carver looked out the window. "Anyway, it's too late for you to start again today. It will be dark soon. You can spend the night here and leave tomorrow at dawn. And when you go, I think King and I will camp right at the roadside for the next four days and nights. If they come after you again, they're almost certain to come this way. For one thing, they'll think you may still be in the cabin. And if you're not, they'll know you must have gone on along this road, since there isn't any other."

So Ellen and Otto ate another meal with Mr. Carver, and when it was over, talked some more about wood sculpture. Mr. Carver showed Otto how to use one of his small, razor-sharp knives. Otto's own hunting knife, he said, was too big and clumsy. Under his direction, Otto succeeded in making a small but respectable wooden cat. Its eyes turned out quite slanted and evil looking.

"That's not the way I wanted them to look," Otto complained.

Mr. Carver laughed. "That's what I meant about wood having a mind of its own." And he gave Otto the knife to keep.

The children made pallets on the floor of the cabin, and they all went to sleep. Ellen woke up frequently, for the floor was hard, and several times she heard the footsteps of the dog King as he walked around the cabin, checking it to make sure all was quiet before returning to his vigil at the road. He was a conscientious dog.

They were up by dawn the next morning. A feeling of urgency had settled over all of them during the night. Mr. Carver had risen first, and had cooked and eaten breakfast while Ellen and Otto still slept. Then, while they ate, he made several trips down to the road. As they packed and shouldered their rucksacks, he returned from the last of these, and they walked down the path together.

Mr. Carver had established a sentry post beside the road, hidden behind some bushes so that anyone approaching would not see it. He had brought down a chair and a sleeping bag. Against a tree near the chair leaned a long-barreled hunting rifle.

About a hundred yards up the road he had also set up an alarm system, ingenious in its simplicity. Across the road at knee height he had stretched a piece of thin black thread. It was hard to see even in the daylight, and would be completely invisible at night. One end was tied to a tree, the other to an iron pail placed on a large stone. Anyone who came up the road at night would inevitably knock the pail over with a loud clang.

One would think that such elaborate precautions would have been reassuring to Ellen and Otto, but the truth is, they had just the opposite effect. The rifle, particularly, seemed ominous. Mr. Carver was evidently taking this very, very seriously; he was now convinced the danger to them was urgent and grave.

The children felt the need to be gone quickly. But first they said goodbye to Mr. Carver and thanked him, and Ellen could not refrain from asking one question:

"Those two statues in your cabin—the two faces. Who are they?"

"I made them about two years ago, because I discovered, though I could hardly believe it, that I was beginning to forget what their faces looked like. Yet remembering the way they looked is one of the things I enjoy most. So, before the memory grew even mistier, I carved the statues. One is Eliza. The other is my wife."

"Someday," he added, "I would like to carve your face, too. When you're safe again and with your aunt, come back and visit me."

"I will," said Ellen.

"I will, too," said Otto.

They walked briskly down the dirt road, heading for the highest pass. As they reached the first bend, Ellen looked back. She saw that Mr. Carver had seated himself in the chair, facing the other way, and King was sitting beside him.

The Broken Road

THEY marched along now in a businesslike style. Their legs had become tuned to the steady pace, and their backs were used to the packs. After they had walked for about three hours, the road resumed its old unpleasant habit, bearing off in a huge arc to the right, and running steadily upward along the massive side of the highest mountain yet. Even this did not bother Ellen as much as it used to. She kept her eyes steadfastly ahead and ignored the steep cliff falling off on their right.

It was nearly midday when Otto, who was walking a few paces ahead, stopped abruptly.

"Hey," he said. "The road's gone."

Ellen came forward to his side, and Richard fluttered to a crag overhead. It was true: for the next hundred feet or so the narrow ledge on which they stood had crumbled away and lay, as a collection of broken boulders, far below them in the valley. There remained only a few jagged outcroppings, not big enough for even a mountain goat to climb on. Ahead, on the other side of this gap, they could see where the road resumed. But the only way to reach it would be to fly.

As if to demonstrate this, Richard flapped his wings, soared along the rocky face of the high cliff, and settled on the very edge where the road began again. It was as if he were saying, "See, it's easy. Just follow me."

Ellen and Otto looked at one another in dismay. What were they to do now?

As far ahead as they could see, which was at least four or five miles along the mountainside, the road continued intact, except for this single gap. Then it curved off to the left and out of sight, into the highest pass. From there on it would be downhill to the highway. They were that close to success.

Ellen took off her rucksack, put it down, and sat on the road forlornly.

"It's gone, all right," she said.

"How do you suppose it happened?"

"A landslide, maybe. Or an earthquake."

"That cliff is so steep. Otherwise we could climb across it."

"But we can't." Just the thought made Ellen dizzy.

"No. We'll have to go back."

"We can't go back. Mr. Carver said himself that he couldn't guard the road forever."

"We can't stay here for long. If they catch us here, we're trapped."

That was a horrifying thought, and another one now occurred to Ellen. Could it be that the stranger, who had walked this way, also knew that the road was out? Was he counting on this to stop them?

"We've *got* to go on somehow."

They sat for a few minutes, thinking painfully, but no ideas at all came to Ellen. Then Otto cried:

"I know how! It's simple!"

His voice was so confident that it automatically brought a surge of relief to Ellen. She was glad Otto had come with her.

"How?" she asked rather humbly.

"Look. We can walk back to where the road first starts out along this cliff. It's only a couple of miles. Here, we can't get off the road—it's too steep. But back there we can. So let's just leave the road, and head through the woods toward the pass."

It *was* simple.

"You're right," she said. "Of course. Let's do it now."

"Shouldn't we eat some lunch first?"

"Let's get to the woods first. I don't like to stop here. It does seem like a trap."

"All right," said Otto agreeably.

They started back immediately. Ellen felt a most urgent desire to get off the road, and quickly. Now that their way was blocked behind them, she kept fearing that she would see, approaching them on the road, a dark figure in the distance. Supposing that somehow the stranger—or someone else, for that matter—had got past Mr. Carver's guard post? She felt like running.

But Otto was less concerned. He kept stopping and staring out over the broad valley far below them, toward the chain of mountains that rose on the other side of it. These were so far off that they shimmered blue and hazy in the distance.

"Hurry," Ellen said when Otto stopped again. "What are you looking at, anyhow?"

"When we first started back, I thought I saw some kind of a big stone building in the woods—way off, over that way." Otto pointed in the general direction of the high pass, but somewhat to the right of it, toward the distant mountains. "But now I can't see it anymore. It must have been just a big gray rock. But it looked too high and straight to be a rock. It looked like a tower."

Ellen paused—very briefly—and looked where he pointed.

"I don't see anything." They walked on. "Anyway, who'd build a building way out there in the middle of the woods?"

"Mr. Carver did."

"A log cabin. That's different. You said a big stone building."

"Well," Otto said, "I said it was probably just a big rock."

"Let's hurry."

They went on, and in about half an hour, to Ellen's vast relief, they were back to the woods, which here reached up from the valley on a steep slope, but a slope they could easily climb down.

Now a new problem came up. Their object, of course, was to walk the whole length of the valley and rejoin the road at the far end, where it went through the pass. But from here they could no longer see the pass. It was completely hidden by the trees.

Ellen stopped. "How will we know which way to go? Once we get into those trees, we'll be lost."

"No we won't," Otto said. "I walk in the woods all the time without any path. I never get lost."

"How do you do it?"

"The easiest way is to watch the sun. Ever since we started on this trip, we've been walking away from the sunrise in the morning and toward the sunset in the evening."

When Ellen thought about it, she realized this was true.

"That means we're heading west," Otto continued. "And that's the way the road was going on the cliff. So we walk toward the sun this afternoon, and away from it tomorrow morning."

"What do we do when it's straight overhead?" Ellen glanced upward. "Like now?"

"We eat lunch."

So they did, as soon as they had walked a few hundred yards down the slope so as to be out of sight of the road. They stepped very carefully here, leaping from one big rock to another where they could, covering their footprints with leaves or pine needles when there were no stones. They left no trail to be seen from the road.

It was pleasant to be back in the forest, though the trees were not quite as big as those they had walked through before, and as a result there was somewhat more underbrush—patches of saplings, bushes and brambles to walk around. Still, they were grateful for the shade, for the sun was hot overhead, and after they ate they rested and looked up at the leaves. They had to wait, as Otto had explained, for the sun to show them which way was west.

Otto knew the names of all the trees. The big one they lay under, with the crooked trunk, tattered bark and feathery fronds was a locust. The massive tall trunk next to it, looking like a gray stone column, was a beech. There were tulip trees, high and graceful and straight, with no low branches; and an aspen, with flat-stemmed leaves that fluttered constantly, even when the other leaves stood still. There were pines and oaks, and one short, wide-branched tree with bark like the scales on a snake: a dogwood.

"I bet Mr. Carver wouldn't work on that wood," Otto said.

"Why not?"

"Too hard. I think it's the hardest wood there is. I tried to whittle some once and it broke my knife blade."

They stood up now. Otto looked at the forest floor, put on his rucksack, helped Ellen with hers, and led the way through the woods.

"You can tell when to go by watching the shadows," he said. "When they start to move, you move the other way." By which he meant, Ellen figured out, that when the sun moves west, the shadows move east.

Otto certainly seemed to know where he was going. He led the way steadily and surely, and Ellen followed him without question. And as the afternoon wore on and the sun moved farther west, she saw that they were indeed following it, and had been all along. In the woods, Richard flew most of the time, fluttering from branch to branch ahead of them rather than riding their shoulders. If only he could speak English a little better, Ellen thought, we could send him up above the treetops. Then he could see the pass and let us know if we're going straight toward it.

In midafternoon they paused by a brook to rest, drink, wash, and refill their water bottle. Then, as they started out again, Otto, who had been silent, said suddenly:

"I really *liked* Mr. Carver. I wish we hadn't had to leave so soon."

"I did, too."

"I wish I had a father like him. He knows all kinds of things. I bet he trained that dog himself."

"I expect he did."

"Anyway, I really am going back to learn woodcarving. I'm going to study drawing at school, and practice at home."

"I thought it was sad," Ellen said. "I mean about his wife and daughter both dying."

"I know what. Maybe he could marry your Aunt Sarah."

"That's silly. They don't even know each other."

"We could introduce them."

"We could, but how do we know they'd fall in love? Anyway, he's a lot older than she is."

"It doesn't matter if the man is older. It's when the women are older that the men won't marry them."

This struck Ellen as a rather cruel way to put it, and also as an unfair situation. Still, she knew it was generally true, or at least it was generally accepted as being true, so she did not argue.

"If they got married," Otto persisted, "Mr. Carver could adopt me for a son. Your Aunt Sarah could adopt you, and we'd be brother and sister."

"But what about your mother?" Ellen asked, and immediately wished she hadn't.

"What?" said Otto, rather absently.

"Nothing."

If Otto was forgetting about Mrs. Fitzpatrick already, it was, after all, what she herself had hoped. But, of course, it might be that he was just easily entranced by his own daydreams. After a while he asked:

"What's it like where she lives?"

"Where who lives?"

"Your Aunt Sarah. Where we're going."

"It's beautiful."

"Yes, but *how?*"

"She's got a great big house, with about thirty rooms in it—a white house. There's a garden behind it, with benches, and then a woods. And behind that there's a hill, a big, wide, low hill, all grassy. That's the Blue Hill. It's a pasture, really. That's where we ride sometimes."

"Ride in what?"

"Ride horses. Aunt Sarah's horse is named Othello— he's black as night. I ride a gray one named Dapper."

"I wish we'd get there. I'd like to ride a horse. Do you suppose she got your postcard by now?"

"I guess so. If she's there." Ellen began to wonder what Aunt Sarah would do when she did get the card. Nothing, probably, at first, since the card said that Ellen was on her way. Aunt Sarah would, right now, be expecting her to arrive any minute. But in a few more days . . . but they should be there by then.

Suppose they weren't? Then, Ellen thought, Aunt Sarah would most likely call the police and start a search. She even had some pictures of Ellen she could show them. But

search where? Along the road between her home and
Oakstable. She wondered whether anyone—perhaps an
attendant at the gas station—had seen her get into the car
with Mr. Gates. That would be a clue for them. If they
tracked her to Mrs. Fitzpatrick's house, of course, then
they would know where to go. But by that time she would
be back down to the main highway, and surely they would
be looking for her there in any case.

They walked on. The ground continued to slope downward, steeply at times, then more gently as they approached the valley floor. The sun moved farther ahead,
and the shadows stretched out behind them. Finally, as the
ground grew almost level underfoot, the sun disappeared
entirely, and they knew it had set behind the mountain
wall toward which they were walking. Sunset comes early
in deep valleys, and the dusk is long.

They kept going a little longer, guided by a small stream
that had come up and joined them, flowing the same way
they were walking. Then it took a sharp bend to the right,
and at this bend they stopped to camp for the night. There
was no cushion of pine needles here, but they collected
piles of dead leaves, and made their blankets comfortable
enough.

It grew quite chilly after sunset, and Otto gathered a
small mountain of firewood, enough to last the night and
more. He made the fire so hot that Ellen's hands and face
turned bright red when she had to cook supper over it:
dried meat and water from the brook, boiled with some
fresh carrots and onions Mr. Carver had given them from
his garden. He had also given them a dozen ears of new
corn. They roasted four of these at the edge of the fire,
leaving the shucks on and turning them frequently so they

would not burn. Richard ate some of the roasted corn, some scraps of meat, and then flew off to find some bugs and berries of his own before it got dark.

When they had eaten everything, Ellen washed the dishes and the cooking pot at the edge of the stream. Then they sat by the fire and stared at the flames, not ready to sleep quite yet, though they were tired.

"I wish I knew how far we've come," Ellen said. That was the advantage of a road. You could see far enough ahead and far enough behind you, most of the time anyway, so you got some idea of your progress. In the woods you couldn't tell at all.

"I bet we're halfway at least."

"How can you tell?"

"Well, one thing—we're not going downhill anymore. Not much, at least. Tomorrow, if we start going uphill, we'll know we're beginning to climb out of the valley."

"It looked so *long* from up on the cliff. I couldn't even guess how many miles."

"I'll tell you what. Tomorrow, after we've walked a little farther, I'll climb a tree and see if I can see the pass. Or the road along the cliff."

"That's a good idea. If we can find a tree that's higher than the rest."

They rolled up in their blankets. Otto went to sleep immediately. Ellen stayed awake a little longer, thinking of the black immensity of the forest around her, listening for sounds but hearing only the occasional rustling of leaves in the wind and the faint swirl of the brook. She was glad of the fire. Most of all she was glad that Otto had come with her. When she finally went to sleep, she did not awaken until morning.

Down the Crevasse

DAYLIGHT came long before sunrise. They had packed their rucksacks and were waiting impatiently before the first red rays finally struggled over the mountain behind them. They lit the treetops, and then slanted down to the forest floor.

Ellen and Otto started walking immediately and fast, for they were eager to finish the journey today if they could. After the first hour or so the last trace of downhill slope ended. They had now definitely reached the bottom of the valley. How long it would continue flat before it started to rise again they did not know. Ellen wished she had studied the shape of the valley more carefully when they had looked at it from the road. She had an idea that it continued level for most of the way, and then rose steeply at the end. But she was not sure.

Otto, who might have been reading her mind, said:

"I'll climb a tree now and see where we are."

They looked until they found a tree that seemed to be taller than any around it—a large beech with a trunk as wide as a door. Otto shed his rucksack, spit on his hands, rubbed them together to make them sticky, and went up like a monkey. Richard followed him, flapping around the edges of the tree while Otto stayed near the trunk. They had played this game before. In thirty seconds Ellen could no longer see either of them.

She stood back and craned her neck, looking upward. Only an occasional faint jarring of leaves showed Otto's progress. But finally Richard erupted from the treetop like a stone from a slingshot, and then the very highest limbs began shaking.

"What do you see?" Ellen called.

"Nothing." His voice floated faintly down through the leaves. "I'm still looking." There was more rustling in the top, and then some more again, as Otto moved around, trying to scan in every direction. Finally he called: "I'm coming down."

A few minutes later he emerged, scrambling down the trunk and landing on his feet, only a little breathless.

"Could you see the pass?"

"No. The tree's not high enough. But I saw one that is. It's much higher than any of the others. Or else it's on a hill."

"Where?"

"That way." He pointed more or less in the direction they had been going, but somewhat off to the right—north.

"How far? Can you climb up it?"

"Yes. Maybe a mile."

Twenty-five minutes and several more tree-climbs later they found it. It was a huge pine, towering a third of its length over everything else around it, and it was, in fact, growing from the top of a low hillock.

"I hate climbing pine trees."

"Why?"

"Sticky pitch."

But he went up anyway. Almost at the top of the tree there was a bare patch of trunk, where all the branches had fallen away—probably struck by lightning—and in perhaps fifteen minutes Ellen saw Otto reach this, clinging like a sailor to a mast, looking as tiny as a puppet. But he shouted down happily:

"I see it! I see it!"

"Which way?"

"That way." He could spare one arm briefly to point like a semaphore in the direction they had been walking.

He pulled the arm back and clung there, still looking.

"I see something else, too."

"What?"

"A line."

"A what?"

"I'm not sure. Wait a minute. I'm coming down."

But he stayed there, staring, for another minute. Then he shinnied down and disappeared into the branches.

When he dropped to the base of the tree a little later his hands were, as he had predicted, covered with brown, gluey pitch.

"We're going the right way. But we're not halfway yet. At least I don't think so." He rubbed his hands in the dirt to get the pitch off, or at least to get some dirt on to make it less sticky.

"What was the other thing?"

"I couldn't tell exactly. Some kind of a line, almost straight across the valley. It might be just a big brook—only it's too straight—or it might be a road. I couldn't see for the trees."

"How far away?"

"Quite a long way. Maybe halfway between here and the end of the valley. It's time for lunch. I wish I could wash."

"Go ahead. The water bottle's full."

"You think it's all right?"

"Only don't use too much."

He used about a third of the water, and some soap, but his hands were still gluey. What he needed was turpentine, or a *lot* of water and some sand. So Ellen peeled his hard-boiled eggs for him, and broke up his hardtack, and he ate them with a fork, getting the handle messy.

When the sun westered again they went on, and in mid-afternoon—about three o'clock—they discovered what the line was. They came on it all of a sudden. With a little bad luck they might have fallen into it.

At some time, centuries ago, the earth had split here, leaving a deep, wide crevasse of stone across the valley. It lay across their path like a straight ditch as wide as a room and two stories deep, with sheer walls of stone. Along the dark bottom a stream flowed silently.

Otto spoke in wonder:

"I never saw anything like that before."

"Neither did I. Except pictures of the Grand Canyon."

"That's out west."

'Yes. And it's a lot deeper than this."

"But people climb down it."

"I guess so. I think they ride donkeys."

"Well," Otto said, "we've got to get across it somehow." He went to the edge and peered down, lying on his stomach so he could lean his head over. "It's pretty steep," he began, "but . . . hey, listen to that!" His words were bouncing around his ears like ping-pong balls, echoing and re-echoing and re-re-echoing from up and down the rock walls.

"I don't hear anything." Ellen was standing too far back.

"Come up closer. You won't fall."

So Ellen nerved herself and looked over the edge too, and heard the echoes. For a while they amused themselves by shouting "Hey!" and counting the number of "heys" that came back—as many as seven, if they shouted loudly enough. But then they got back to the seriousness of the problem.

"We've got to climb down it," Otto said, "and cross the stream and climb up the other side. I think I can do it. I see some handholds."

"Well I can't," Ellen said. "I know I can't. It's too steep."

"If only we had a rope."

"But we don't."

"I know what!"

"What?"

"A grapevine."

They had passed many of these—great, long, strong wild cords hanging from the tops of trees—and had swung on some of them. But it was one thing to swing on a vine close to the ground, and another to descend on one into a deep crevasse with a rock bottom.

"Suppose it breaks?"

"We can test it first."

"But even if we did get to the bottom that way, how do we get up the other side?"

"We'll just have to walk along the bottom until we find a place where we can climb up."

Finally they worked out a plan. They would walk along the edge of the crevasse, looking in the trees for a suitable grapevine—they had seen some nearly as thick as their wrists, and that was the kind they wanted. But as they walked they would also watch for places in the opposite wall that looked climbable. And who knows? Ellen thought hopefully, they might even find a section where the walls weren't as steep on either side, and then they could walk down.

The crevasse struck across their westerly course almost due north and south, that is, leading off to their right and to their left. Whichever way they followed it would take them out of their way. But after some study of directions, shadows and the sun, they decided that if they went north they would be making at least a little forward progress, for that way it seemed to angle slightly to the west. So they turned right, toward the distant mountains they had seen from the cliff.

They found a strong and supple grapevine soon enough. They tested it for strength this way: While the vine still hung from the tree, Otto climbed up, hand over hand, until he was six feet in the air. Then Ellen climbed after him until she, too, was off the ground, and the vine was supporting both of them at once. If it would hold their combined weights, they reasoned, surely it would be strong enough to hold them one at a time as they climbed down the crevasse. Having made sure of its strength, Otto then went up the tree and cut the vine off at the top, where its small brown tendrils clung to the trunk. They coiled it like a lasso and carried it along.

Now to find a place where they could climb up the far side. They walked a mile, two miles, then three. They had to go slowly, so they could study the crevasse as they went.

At about the third mile, Richard began to behave in a strange manner. Ellen noticed it first, because he had lit on her shoulder, gripping it harder than usual.

"Look at Richard. He's shaking all over."

Otto turned. Not only was Richard trembling, but his feathers, normally sleek and shiny, were rumpled in disorder.

"He looks sick. Poor Richard."

Otto held out his hand, but Richard, instead of lighting on his finger, gave a high, quavering cry and flew away. He flew hard, and disappeared over the trees, back in the direction they had come from.

"I wonder what's wrong," Otto said. "He never did that before."

"Could someone be following us?"

"No. He'd make more noise. Something's the matter with him."

They went on. Richard reappeared in about fifteen minutes, looking sicker than ever. He settled on Otto's shoulder, and they could hear him muttering sadly to himself, "Poor Richard . . . poor Richard." He stayed only a few seconds, and then flew off again in the same direction as before.

"Either he's sick," Otto said, "or there's something here he doesn't like."

"Or he's watching something back there."

"I don't think so. He acts as if he just can't stand to stay in one place."

"I wonder why?"

"I don't know. But birds feel things we don't. Something is scaring him. Something in the air."

Still, they had to go on; all they could do was hope that Richard would get over it. And then, at about the fifth mile, they saw something that made them forget all about him, for the moment at least.

To their enormous joy, they had found a place where the wall on the far side of the crevasse was not sheer. It was, in fact, a jumbled mess. A dark fissure led back into it, and great boulders lay strewn about, as if a giant had smashed it with a gargantuan sledgehammer. The boulders were jagged and rough, with plenty of hand and footholds; they formed a sort of stairway to the top which looked, from where they stood, easily climbable.

Their vine-rope, looped around a big tree and knotted firmly, reached easily to the bottom of the crevasse with feet to spare. They tied their rucksacks to it and lowered them first, to be free of the extra weight.

Then Otto went down, lowering himself quickly hand over hand as Ellen watched from above.

"Come on down," he shouted from the bottom. "It's easy." And the echoes called out ". . . easy-easy-easy-

easy-easy . . ."

But for Ellen it was not easy. She was terrified. "Don't look down"—the warning came to her from something she had read long ago. Grimly she turned around and crawled herself backward until her feet, then her legs, then her waist were over the edge. She gripped the vine.

"If it were only four feet down, " she told herself, "you'd think nothing of it. Pretend it's only four feet." And her head disappeared over the side.

The vine scored her hands. The stone wall inched up past her eyes. She tried to get her feet around the vine as Otto had done, but they could not find it, and she dared not look. Halfway down—was she halfway?—her arms began to ache furiously. A little farther, and her knee banged hard against a sharp point of stone. She kicked instinctively away from it, and began to sway. Her hands slipped, and she slid, slithered and fell the rest of the way.

She was sitting on the bottom, and Otto was beside her. "You made it. You're all right."

But she was not all right. The fall had not been much—only a few feet—but when she landed her weak ankle had wrenched hideously under her.

She sat, clasping it with both hands. She had turned very pale.

"I've got to be sick," she said, and was.

The Cave

WHEN Ellen had stopped being sick, they inspected her ankle. There were no bones sticking out, or bulging where they shouldn't, so they decided that it was not broken. But it hurt dreadfully, and when she tried, very cautiously, to stand on it, she turned pale again and sat down quickly.

"I can't walk," she said.

"You've sprained it."

"I must have. It's the same ankle I hurt before. I suppose it was still weak."

"As long as it isn't broken, it will heal."

"Yes, but when?"

"We'll just have to rest awhile and see."

That was the trouble. Neither of them knew much about sprained ankles, though Ellen could remember vaguely when her brother David had sprained his wrist playing football a couple of years before. He had gone to

133

the doctor and come home with his arm in a sling.

In a little while her ankle began to swell alarmingly.

"I think we're supposed to put hot compresses on it."

"How do you do that?"

"You heat up some water. Then you soak a towel in it and put it on." Or was it cold compresses? Ellen was not sure.

Otto said: "There's plenty of water in the brook. But I'll have to get some wood to make a fire. There's none down here."

Since her fall, Ellen had scarcely looked around her. They were in the flat bottom of the crevasse, a rock corridor stretching in both directions as far as she could see, the walls and the slit of sky above them growing closer and narrower the farther off she looked, like railroad tracks meeting in the distance. Strangely enough, when they spoke down here at the bottom, there was scarcely any echo at all.

The floor she sat on was clean gray stone, and slanted down toward the far wall. Along that wall ran the stream, perhaps four feet wide, looking only slightly less dark and mysterious from here than it had from above. From wall to wall was, at a guess, about twelve feet. On the near wall, just behind her, hung the grapevine they had climbed down.

A little way downstream, toward the distant mountains, the water broke with a gurgle against the scarred gray face of a boulder, the first of the jumbled rocks they had seen from the forest edge. Amid the boulders, she remembered, was the cleft in the wall.

And it was true: There was scarcely a twig of wood to

be seen anywhere. There were no trees down here, nor any growing thing, and naturally when the stream flooded in the spring it would wash away any boughs that happened to fall from the trees above.

"I've got to climb out of here anyway," Otto said. "When I get to the top, I'll bring some wood back. We can make a fire right here."

He squirmed his way up the first boulder with no trouble and stood on top of it looking around. Then, with a wave of his hand he disappeared behind it. Ellen sat, watching her ankle, wondering when it would stop hurting; then she heard a shout from above her, looked up, and there was Otto's face looking down at her from the top of the crevasse—on the far side, the side they had to gain.

"I'm getting some wood," he called. "I'll throw it down."

"Was it hard to climb?"

"It's nothing. It was fun. I'll tell you when I come back. I've got a surprise for you."

His head disappeared, and in a moment a cascade of firewood began pouring over the edge about twenty feet upstream from where Ellen sat. It kept coming for fifteen minutes, and Otto must have been working like a bulldozer, because scarcely a second passed that another big branch did not come crashing down. Then his head popped over the side again.

"Does that look like enough?"

Ellen looked at the pile that had risen against the stone wall.

"Yes. There's plenty."

"I'm coming down."

But it was a few more minutes before he reappeared, wading around the boulder through the stream. He had taken time to cut what he carried in his hand: a sturdy green bough that was bent in a natural L-shape at one end. He handed it to her.

"Here. I'll cut another one the next time I go up."

"What's it for?"

"A crutch. But you'll need two."

Ellen looked at it with some dismay.

"But I can't walk all that way with crutches. I don't even know how."

"I know that." He started arranging the sticks for a fire. "But you might be able to walk a little way."

"But what's the use?"

"Because I found a good place for us to camp. Until your ankle gets better."

"What kind of a place?"

"That's the surprise. Wait till you see it."

He would say no more. He lit the fire, filled the pot with water and put it on to heat: They tested it by putting their wrists in, and when it was just uncomfortably hot they took it off the fire.

They had no towel, of course, but Otto peeled off his shirt, rolled it up and dipped it in the water.

"It needed washing anyway," he said cheerfully.

They applied hot compresses steadily for the next half-hour or so, and somewhat to the surprise of both, the treatment seemed to work. Although the swelling did not go down, neither did it increase; the pain eased, and most important, Ellen's alarm subsided.

After Otto had climbed the wall again and cut her another crutch, she was even persuaded to try a few hobbling steps. It was not very difficult, though she could only go a little way at a time because her arms and shoulders got tired. But she quickly learned to rest by leaning slightly forward, dividing her weight between the crutches and her good leg. She also learned to keep the knee of her other leg bent, so that her sore ankle stayed well off the ground. Otto stood close at hand while she practiced, ready to dash in and catch her if she stumbled.

Finally she let go the crutches and sank to the ground, puffing a little but pleased with herself for having learned to use them.

"Now I'll rest a while. Then I want to see the surprise. How far is it?"

"Just a little way—around on the other side of that boulder."

"I can't climb over it. I'll have to go in the stream."

"That's all right. It's only about three inches deep, and the bottom's flat."

Wading through a stream over a slippery bottom on homemade crutches is not the best therapy for a sprained ankle. Ellen had to stop and rest eleven times on the way; once one crutch slipped away, but Otto's shoulder was there to grab, and they got the crutch back somehow before it floated away downstream. And then they were around the boulder, and Ellen was back on dry land.

In front of them was the cleft in the rock wall they had seen from above. Otto, who had already been through it, led the way impatiently as Ellen labored along behind. She made her way slowly, one small step at a time, up the slight incline that led from the stream bed. The cleft looked like a doorway in a Gothic cathedral, and it was just wide enough for her crutches. She went into it, and found herself in a magic room.

It was a cave, but like no cave she had ever heard of, for it was lit with flashing diamonds.

She gasped in delight, while Otto hopped around her on one foot.

"I *told* you I had a surprise."

The cave had a front door and a back door. The back door, which they had just entered, faced east and led to the stream, an inexhaustible water supply. The front door faced west and led, after a rocky climb, to the forest, an inexhaustible wood supply.

Through this western door poured a gay shaft of late afternoon sunlight. It struck the inside wall of the cave and shattered into a thousand spears of brilliance—mostly white, but mixed faintly with blue, red, orange and yellow. For the walls of the cave, made of sandstone, had become mixed with another kind of stone—tiny crystals as clear as glass, not really diamonds, but almost as shiny. Ellen could even remember their name; her father had told her once when she found a piece of this same kind of stone in the country.

"Quartzite."

"What?"

"Quartzite. That's what those shiny stones are. Aren't they beautiful?"

"I knew you'd like it. And it's got three rooms."

Not really three rooms, but the cave floor was split into three levels, like some modern houses. As you walked from the back door to the front you came to a ledge of stone, waist-high, and when you clambered up that you stood on the second level, looking down at where you had just been. Farther along was another ledge and a third section, higher than the second. So it had the effect of three rooms, even without partitions. All in all, the cave was nearly as big as a small house. It was dry and cool, and because of its shining walls, astonishingly light.

Otto went back and got their rucksacks; then he moved the stack of firewood to the cave, since it was nearly suppertime. They discovered there was a perpetual draft, a whisper of air so slight you could feel it only faintly on your ears when you stood in either doorway. It blew in the front door and out the back, keeping the atmosphere from getting the dank smell that most caves have.

And it meant that the place to build the fire was inside the cave near the back door; all the smoke blew out as neatly as if it were rising up a chimney.

Otto got it lit just in time. As the sun sank in the West, the shaft of light through the front door climbed higher up the wall, shrank to half its size, then a quarter, and then flicked out altogether, as if someone had turned a switch. And they were in the dark: there is no twilight in caves.

The fluttering firelight illuminated only the lowest level of the wall, and that only dimly in a deep ruby red. Beyond the first ledge the cave was dark; at the far end they could barely make out the faint gray silhouette of the front door, and that was all.

Otto still had to go out into the woods to get some bedding; for the floor of the cave was hard rock, and unlike the walls, coal-black except for some patches of gravelly sand. What he wanted was a flashlight, but they had none. He was getting ready to grope his way through the blackness into the outer twilight when he had an idea.

"A pine knot," he said.

"What's that?"

"For a light. They're as good as lanterns. My mother uses them to start the fire." In the stack of firewood he found a knobby pine branch shaped like a club, with a cluster of knots at the thick end where branches had once grown out. He thrust this end into the fire, and when he pulled it out he had a fine flaming torch, good for perhaps half an hour. Holding this high above his head he set off through the cave, casting monstrous leaping shadows on the walls.

In the morning, when the sunlight stabbed through the back door and the cave was light again, they had to face two hard facts: Ellen's ankle seemed no better at all, and their food was running low.

The night before, after Otto had come in with a huge armload of soft-needled pine boughs for bedding, they had cooked and eaten almost half of their meat.

Now they took the food they had left and divided it into little piles, each one representing a meal. It did not come out even: by splitting the meat into very skimpy portions, they had enough for two dinners, whereas there was quite a lot of hardtack—enough for five or six days; there were three eggs apiece—three breakfasts; there were three ears of corn and two carrots.

"I wish it would get better," Ellen said, looking at her misshapen ankle, which was as big around as a grapefruit, and which she could not move at all without a pain worse than a toothache.

"Don't worry. It will." Otto was acquiring a bedside manner. "The only thing is, we don't know how soon."

"We should put some more compresses on it."

They revived the breakfast fire, and Otto went shirtless again. They really worked hard and seriously at it for more than an hour, at the end of which the ankle was no smaller at all, but had turned a very bright red. Was that a good sign or bad? They did not know.

At lunchtime Ellen said, "We'll have to go on starvation rations."

"I guess so."

"Let's say that my ankle won't heal for two more days."

"How do you know?"

"Don't you see? We have to *plan* as if it might not. Because otherwise, if it doesn't we'll run out of food."

Otto thought this over rather gloomily. "All right," he said. "But I wish I didn't get so hungry."

"We had meat for dinner last night, so tonight we won't eat any. Then we'll have some for tomorrow night, and still have enough left for one meal after we start again."

After lunch Ellen felt sleepy. Her inflamed ankle and all the hot compresses had made her feverish, and her head ached. She lay in her blanket on the pine needles and fell asleep. She slept a long time, for when she awoke the sunlight through the front door was already beginning to climb the wall. Otto was nowhere to be seen, and neither was his rucksack, though its contents were there, dumped in a heap beside his pallet.

He must have gone for wood, Ellen thought. But why would he take his rucksack? She pondered this for a moment, but could think of no answer. Then she thought of her own rucksack, with her handbag in it, and the silver crown. She had not even looked at it since she left Mrs. Fitzpatrick's house.

The bag lay within reach. She opened it, took the crown out, and saw to her astonishment that it had changed. The little blue stones set in the silver, which formerly had sparkled and twinkled like stars, now glowed with a steady blue-white light. It was a calm sort of light, as unwavering as an electric bulb, and many, many times brighter than before.

Ellen looked at it dumfounded. Could it have something to do with the light in the cave? She turned to the bright sunspot on the wall, now a third of the way up to the ceiling. It was, as always, glistening, dancing and flickering with a thousand shifting spears of light. And that *should,* if anything, make the crown sparkle all the more in its reflection. No, that could not be the cause.

The glow seemed almost as if it came from some sort of energy, like a battery. From radioactivity, perhaps? Or was the cave charged with electricity?

Ellen tried an experiment. She got back on her pallet with the crown in her hand, and pulled the blanket up over her head. Under the cover, completely dark, the stones still glowed steadily, looking brighter than ever, turning her hand and even the underside of the blanket faintly blue. So it was not reflection from the cave. She could think of no explanation at all.

She threw back the blanket and, slipping the crown over her wrist like a bracelet, hobbled with her crutches over to the ledge that led to the central section of the cave. With some careful maneuvering she managed to seat herself on this, facing the door—the back door—her feet dangling not quite to the floor. Then she put the crown on her head.

The effect was magical. She could feel the glow of the stones, or whatever power was causing them to glow, pass through her head—through her brain. It would have been frightening, except that it was so obviously, so surely, so beyond question, *good*.

It was, she thought, like a gentle comb going through her mind, straightening out the thoughts and undoing the tangles. She had a feeling of serenity and strength, of sweetness and sureness, that she had never known before. It did not make her ankle any better at all, nor her stomach any less empty, but it made her feel that hunger and a sore ankle are, after all, not so important; they will pass eventually. They became, somehow, remote.

It turned the cave into—what? Not a castle, but a chapel. The sunlight on the wall was a stained glass window, and through the pointed doorway would come, in a few minutes, an archbishop in a tall medieval hat, or perhaps a saint with a golden halo. The wash of the brook behind the door reached her ears as faint music, a hushed, sustained chord sung by a far-off choir.

She was suddenly aware of Otto standing in front of her, staring at her entranced but also frightened.

"Are you all right?" he asked anxiously.

She took off the crown and the music stopped.

"Yes, I'm fine. Only hungry."

"You looked so funny. Sort of pale and, well . . . hypnotized."

"Did I? I felt that way, too. Not pale, I mean, but strange. It's the crown that does it. Here, you try it."

But when Otto put the crown on, it had no effect on him. He felt its light weight on his forehead, but nothing more.

"It doesn't work with me," he said sadly. "I didn't think it would . . . Look at the stones!"

"I know. They've changed."

"They look electric. Like a radium dial."

"Radium dials aren't electric."

"You know what they really look like?"

"What?"

"Lightning bugs, only they don't turn off."

And that was, in fact, an apt description of the light the stones gave off, though they were much smaller than a lightning bug.

"It's got something to do with this place," Otto said.

"How do you mean?"

"I mean there's something funny about this whole part of the woods. When I went out, I climbed some trees to look for birds' eggs. They're good to eat if you can find fresh ones. And you know what? There aren't any birds here at all. No birds, no nests, no eggs."

And they both thought of Richard. They had not seen him—beak, claw nor feather—since they came down the crevasse.

Otto the Provider

I F there were no birds, there were no eggs; but with no birds to eat them, there were berries in fantastic abundance. Otto's rucksack was loaded with them. He dumped them out carefully on a clean rocky part of the floor: blueberries, blackberries, raspberries, wild cherries, and even some wild grapes, which were, however, too green to eat.

"They don't fill you up much," he said, "but they're good for dessert."

Otto did not think highly of starvation rations, and he had several plans to do something about them. He said no more at the moment, but the berries were only a beginning. Still, they helped to make bearable the meatless and meager dinner, and there was a big pile left over for breakfast.

The next day passed, and the second day began, with no sign that Ellen would be able to walk that day, or even soon.

They had breakfast early, and as soon as it was done, and the dishes cleaned up, Otto climbed the steep rocky path out of the crevasse and into the woods.

Ellen, watching him leave, was worried. In a few minutes she would put the crown on her head, and then, she knew, her troubles would become quite small and remote. But for the moment she felt she *ought* to worry. If their situation was not quite desperate, it bordered on it. Their meat was completely gone now, and while there was still a fair amount of bread left, with nothing else to eat it could not last long. And then what?

The worst of it was the knowledge that it was all her fault. Otto had gone down the crevasse wall easily and fearlessly—easily *because* fearlessly. But she had been a coward; her nerve had failed; her terror had made her lose control, and now they were stuck—three days already, and who could say how many more?

She worried about her Aunt Sarah. She must have received the postcard long ago. Or had she ever received it? If she had, was she searching for them? Not *them*—Aunt Sarah could know nothing of Otto. And how could she search, without the vaguest idea of where to look? Or had she even been at home when the postcard arrived? She might have been traveling—she might still be traveling—without any idea that Ellen was in trouble.

And last—what about the man in black, and the green hoods? They might, even now, be surrounding the cave, closing in from the woods, moving stealthily up the crevasse. She did not really think this was likely, however; the valley was so vast—and if their tracks had been found, surely they would have been caught before now.

Each day that passed made discovery less likely. Or so she must hope.

She got her crutches and her crown, limped over to the ledge and sat down facing the door. She put the crown on her head.

When Otto returned just before lunchtime she was still sitting there. This was the third time he had found her this way: sitting without any movement at all, a rapt, trance-like expression on her face, not smiling but pale and serene, staring at the sunlit cleft of the back door, and listening to some beautiful sound he could not hear.

When she saw him she took the crown off, and Otto smiled broadly in anticipation. He was holding both hands behind his back. Now he held them out. In one he had, by the ears, a rabbit; in the other, by the tail, a squirrel.

Ellen touched the rabbit with one hand; it was still warm, soft and furry. She did not touch the squirrel, which was rather bloody.

"Poor little things," she said. "Are they dead? How did you catch them?"

" 'Poor little things' will make us four good dinners. I got the rabbit with a deadfall. I got the squirrel with my knife."

"What's a deadfall?"

"A trap. You prop up a rock with two sticks. One holds it up. The other one is the trigger. I learned it from a hunting magazine. I put a little bit of carrot on the trigger stick. Rabbit tries to eat the carrot—whump!—down comes the rock. I've another one set, too."

"It's lucky we didn't eat the carrots."

"I took them a couple of days ago—just in case. You never even noticed. I've still got most of them left. You only need a little bit for bait."

Ellen still felt she should protest killing the small, furry creatures. But the thought of having meat to eat again weakened her conscience, and a half-hour later when the rabbit, cleaned and skinned, was sizzling on a spit of green wood over the fire, the smell killed whatever qualms she had left.

It tasted like chicken.

"Only better," Otto said.

"And tougher," Ellen added.

So their food supply was replenished, temporarily at least. They had no assurance, of course, that this would continue. And indeed for the next two days, though he went out morning and afternoon, Otto came back empty-handed. To his annoyance, some bigger animal, probably a groundhog, raided one of his deadfalls, ate the precious bit of carrot and managed to struggle out from under the rock. Otto took to roaming farther and farther as he hunted.

Ellen's ankle was now definitely improving. The swelling had gone down noticeably, but more important, she could wiggle her foot from side to side without its hurting so much. By the afternoon of the seventh day she was actually able to half-hop, half-walk a few steps without the crutches. But a few steps were all, and she had to crawl back on her hands and knees. She felt extremely proud of herself, and waited impatiently for Otto to come back.

He had been away since morning, hunting; this day, for the first time, he had not even returned for lunch, but had taken a scrap of cold meat and a piece of bread with him. Ellen had sat for hours wearing the crown, listening to the strange, distant music it produced in her mind, feeling the peace it brought her.

Once during this time, while she was wearing the crown, she had a strange vision. Perhaps it was a dream; possibly she fell asleep as she sat motionless on the ledge, half hypnotized by the bright doorway and the flickering sparkle of the wall. She felt, suddenly, that she was looking at her father, straight into his eyes, and he was looking back at her, but not seeing her. She could see his face only dimly, for it was in shadow, in a dark room, but she could not mistake his eyes. She thought she saw him speak, but could not hear what he said. Then, without wanting to, she looked away, at another part of the room, and she realized that she was seeing through someone else's eyes, for she could not control the direction in which she looked. She thought she could perceive other figures in the room, and, high up in the dark ceiling, a very small, very dim light. Then she was looking back at her father again, so close she could almost touch him. She tried to call out, but the instant she did the whole vision flickered and vanished, as if she had tried to cry out in a dream and woke herself up instead.

Since she was wearing the crown, she did not feel distressed at this, but wondered calmly what it was she had seen, and through whose eyes. Her father was dead; was he still, then, existing somewhere, seeing and looking the same as before? But then why in such a dark, gloomy chamber? Or were there, after all, such things as ghosts—had she seen her father's spirit?

Not only did the vision disappear; a minute later, when she removed the crown, her memory of it clouded, and in a few seconds she had forgotten it entirely. It was lonely in the cave, and she wished she had someone to talk to, or a book to read. She wished Otto would come, so she could show him how she could walk.

When Otto did return, it was almost dark, and he was so close to exploding that she had no chance to walk. He had made a tremendous discovery.

"You remember the big stone building I saw?"

"From the cliff?"

"When we were walking back. Well, it was real. I found it."

"You said it was just a big rock."

"I said it *must* be just a big rock, but it isn't. It's a building as big as a fort."

"Does anybody live there?"

"Kids—mostly boys. I think it must be some kind of a school. Or maybe a camp."

"Didn't you ask them?"

"No. I didn't go close enough. There's a high fence all the way around it, a *very* high fence, with barbed wire on top, about a half-mile away from the building. On the front side there's a big stone wall."

"But there must be a gate, with a bell or something."

"There is, in the front, but I didn't ring it."

"Why not?"

"I was scared."

"Scared of a *school?*"

"You would be, too." Otto did not admit lightly to being frightened. "There's something . . . well, funny about it. Something wrong."

"You mean about the building?"

"The building is almost black, with towers on it, like a castle. And hardly any windows. But it's not just that. There are these black paths, like driveways, all around the grounds inside the fence."

"What's wrong with that? Most roads are black."

"Wait. I was watching from the edge of the woods, and a bunch of kids came walking along the path. Not one of them ever said a word. They just marched in a straight line, like dead people. And there was a man with them in black clothes. He was dressed exactly like the stranger."

"You mean with the green stripes and everything?"

"Yes. And the kids were dressed in black, too—sort of a uniform."

"The man—*was* he the stranger? The same one?"

"No. He was shorter. And his face was different."

"Where is this place, anyway? How far away?"

"That way. Maybe seven or eight miles." Otto pointed downstream, in the general direction the crevasse and the brook ran. "I'm not sure about the distance. It took me half the day to get there, but I was hunting. Coming straight back, it took about two hours—maybe less, but I was hurrying."

This was the most puzzling development yet. It meant, or it seemed to mean, that the stranger, who had been pursuing them from behind, had actually come from ahead of them. That is, if he did really come from this

strange, fenced-in place. It was barely possible, of course
—but most unlikely—that the similarity in costumes was
just coincidence. Could this, then, be the "headquarters"
they had talked about?

"I wish I could see it," Ellen said. "Who do you suppose the children are?"

"I think they're captives."

"Captives?"

"I don't think they can get out. Otherwise, why should
there be such a high fence?"

"Maybe to keep other people from coming in. That's
what most fences are for. Except in prisons. Maybe it *is* a
prison, or a reform school."

"I could get in," Otto said. "I thought of it. Wire fences
are easy to climb."

"You shouldn't go in," Ellen said quickly. "Otto, *please*
don't try. You were right to be scared. You don't know
what's in there."

"We're almost out of food again," Otto said. This
sounded as if he were changing the subject, and he said no
more about it.

"We have enough for dinner," Ellen said, "and for
breakfast tomorrow. And look—I can. walk without my
crutches." She laid the crutches down, took five slow,
shaky steps away from them, turned, and walked back—
ten steps in all.

"That's *good*," Otto said, as enthusiastically as he
could. But it was all too apparent to both of them that it
was going to be at least two or three more days before
she could begin the long journey over the pass.

The Dark Castle

OTTO was gone all the next day. He returned just before dark, empty-handed except for berries, gloomy and rather preoccupied. He built a fire as usual, but only for warmth and whatever cheer it might bring. There was nothing more to cook. Their supper was a cold one; it consisted of the last few scraps of bread and some berries. They had reached the end of their food.

There was only one cheerful thing. Ellen's ankle continued to improve; she had, in fact, walked without her crutches all the way to the brook and bathed it, and herself, in the cool, dark water. She had barely made it back, however, and afterward the ankle ached quite a lot. Yet she was sure she had done it no harm. She did not tell Otto that it hurt. Her stomach, after the small meal, felt empty and uncomfortable; she was sure that Otto, having hunted all day, must be far hungrier than she. Yet he did not complain; at least, not exactly.

"When we get out of here," he said, "when we get to the highway, I hope we come out near a hamburger stand. I'm going to order six hamburgers with ketchup, rolls, onions, potato chips, and cokes. And pie. Chocolate pie, and eat them all. I don't care if I can't pay. I'll eat them before they find out."

"I can pay. I still have more than a dollar."

"Yes, but you'll want some, too. A dollar isn't enough."

"They'll arrest you."

"I don't care. They have to feed you in jail. And you and Aunt Sarah can come and bail me out."

"If only I can find her. I hope she's *there*."

For some reason, thinking about Aunt Sarah made something in Ellen's mind roll back, and she suddenly remembered the dream of her father. She described it to Otto.

"And the strange thing about it," she said, "is that I didn't feel asleep at all, and when it ended, I didn't feel as if I were waking up."

"Maybe it wasn't a real dream. It doesn't sound like a dream. Maybe it was telepathy."

"How could it be?"

"He might be still alive. I bet he is."

"He isn't alive," Ellen said. "He couldn't be. The fireman said so. Anyway, you didn't see the house."

"Then you must have seen heaven. Maybe when you put the crown on, you can see heaven."

"Heaven wouldn't be so dark." She lay down and pulled the blanket around her. "It was only a dream." With that she was asleep.

When Ellen awoke the next morning, Otto was not there. She was not particularly surprised, since there was nothing for breakfast except a small pile of berries left over from the night before. She assumed that he had awakened earlier and gone hunting, or at least gone to gather some more berries. He had told her that early morning was the best time of day for hunting.

So she ate the berries, and then, without using her crutches, walked quite easily down to the brook to get a drink of water and to wash her face. Of course she was wobbly, and she limped, but she did not hurt. After she washed, she went back to the cave and waited for an hour or so, expecting Otto any minute—she hoped with a rabbit in each hand, but at least with more berries. But he did not come. All day she waited.

By nightfall he still had not returned, and she had begun to worry. Could he have gotten lost? She could hardly believe that, knowing how easily he found his way in the woods. Had he just hunted, hungry as he was—hungry as they both were—much farther than usual, not realizing how far he had gone? If so, he should be back soon, since he could not hunt in the dark.

Suppertime came and went. She was hideously empty, and there was not so much as a green berry left. Since Otto was not there, she built the fire herself; she kept it small, because the wood supply was low. It would be easy enough to build it bigger if he came back with some game. She felt thoroughly miserable, a little frightened, but most of all worried about Otto himself. For a dreadful suspicion had begun to work its way through her mind.

Eventually she fell asleep, and into her sleep crept a
repeating nightmare that woke her up trembling each time
she dreamed it. Each time she woke she looked through
the dim firelight at Otto's blanket, and each time it was
still empty.

In her nightmare Otto was lost, not in the woods but
wandering in an endless maze of dark corridors of stone,
inside the black castle. He could not get out, for all the
doors were locked. At the end of each dream he turned a
corner, and there before him stood a tall figure in black,
wearing a green mask. And it was Otto's voice, calling for
help, that woke her up.

In the morning Ellen knew that the time had come to
stop worrying and start thinking. She was sure now that
Otto was not coming back, and she was quite sure she
knew why. She went over in her mind some of the things
he had said when they talked about the castle, or prison,
or whatever it was. "I could get in," he had said, and,
"Wire fences are easy to climb." And then almost immediately he had talked about food. Ellen could put two and
two together. She realized of course, that she might be
wrong.

Assuming that she was right—then what? She could not
stay here; she would starve. But could she walk well
enough to leave? She tried a few steps and decided that
she could. She should be able to make a few miles each
day, at least. She wondered how long a person could keep
walking without food—or without any food but berries.

Having thought this far, the next question was: where
should she go?

Finally she worked out a plan; and having decided what to do, she wasted no time starting. She was terribly hungry, and at least she could eat some berries along the way.

She packed her rucksack with her own things and discovered—since there was no food to pack—that she had room for Otto's blanket, too, so she put that in just in case. She was careful to take all the matches; there were not many left, and she filled the water bottle from the brook. When everything was ready, she put the rucksack on and climbed up the first ledge, then the second, and walked toward the front door.

But just before she reached it she stopped, as if she had remembered something. She looked around her, considering. Then she walked over to one side of the cave, in the shadow, studying the ground. She dug the toe of her shoe into a gravelly part of the floor, pushing the gravel to one side, still thinking. She slipped off the rucksack, knelt down, opened it, and took out the crown. Using her fingers and then, when the hard stones tore her nails, a knife from her rucksack to help, she dug a hole six inches deep. She folded the crown into the smallest possible shape, placed it at the bottom of the hole, and buried it. She smoothed the gravel carefully over the top, so the hole became instantly invisible. Then she took the knife and on the wall directly over the crown she scratched a small "X" to mark the spot.

Outside the front door of the cave she saw the rocks where Otto had climbed in and out of the crevasse. They were not so formidable as she had feared; it was rather like climbing the steps of a pyramid—you could take them one at a time. Depending more on her knees than her feet, she scrambled to the top easily enough and found herself in the silent, birdless forest.

But the rest of the way was like a bad dream, and got steadily worse. Within a half mile she knew that her ankle was not nearly as strong as she had thought. Perhaps part of the trouble was the extra weight of the rucksack. Her limp deteriorated into a painful hobble, and she had to stop and rest, leaning against a tree, after every few steps. Still she kept going, a few yards at a time, and she did find some berries and ate them.

The rain came on not as a storm but as a slow, chill, foggy drizzle that ran down her neck, soaked her shoes, and made her slacks stick wetly to her legs. It turned the ground slippery underfoot, slowing her progress still further. Worst of all, it hid the sun, which she needed to guide her. In order to keep from getting completely lost, she had to stay near the edge of the crevasse, forcing her way through thickets rather than detouring around them. By noon she felt close to despair; she wanted to give up and go back to the cave. There at least she would be dry; she could sit before the fire and get warm. But if she did that, if she gave up, she would starve. She went on.

By mid-afternoon she could walk no farther. She slumped down on a fallen log under a huge oak tree, hoping that its branches would keep off at least some of the rain. Her hair hung lank and wet around her temples; her clothing dripped, and after she had sat still for a few minutes she began to shiver. The only warm part of her was her lame ankle, which throbbed and ached and burned.

She should, she knew, build a fire. But how build a fire

when every leaf, every twig was soaked and soggy? Then another thought came to her. If she could not light a fire, she might at least make a shelter from the rain: she had two blankets; she would make a tent of one and roll up under it in the other.

She remembered how she and David, when they lived in the country, had made blanket tents. The easiest way was to find a long, low tree limb parallel to the ground, hang the blanket over it and put a stone on each corner.

So, after a minute or two, she got painfully to her feet and started around the big bole of the oak tree to see if, by luck, it had such a branch. And then she discovered, to her relief, that she did not need to make a tent after all. Halfway around the tree she found that the trunk, as big as a dining room table, was hollow—or at least more than half hollow. An opening like a wide door led into it, and the floor inside was deep with brown oak leaves. She stepped in and felt the dry warmth of the tree enclose her like an embrace.

She spread one blanket, folded double, over the leaves. Then she pulled off her wet slacks, shirt, shoes and socks and spread them beside it to dry. She rolled herself in the other blanket and lay down. In ninety seconds she was asleep.

When she awoke it was still light enough to see, though just barely, and she heard a small rustling in the leaves near the entrance to the hollow. She lay still, moving only her eyes to look. It was a chipmunk, a gay little animal hardly bigger than a mouse, striped brown and white and black. He, too, had come in out of the rain. He sat up on his back legs like a squirrel and nibbled something he held in his forepaws. It looked like a piece of bread. Bread? In the forest? How could it be? Then, as Ellen watched, the chipmunk finished the bit he was eating, darted out the door and came back in a minute with a bigger piece—a mushroom.

Ellen rolled over so she could see better. The leaves rustled under her. The chipmunk looked at her, made a tentative hop toward the door, and waited, watching her. He did not want to go back out in the rain unless he had to. Ellen moved again, slowly. The chipmunk stayed where he was. Gradually she inched herself to where she could see out the door. The chipmunk, quite calmly, began to eat again. Obviously this big, sluggish creature was not going to hurt him.

Through the door Ellen could now see where he had found his meal. Back perhaps thirty feet stood a broken-off tree trunk, a tall, jagged stump. And out of it, sides and top, grew a small forest of the white, crescent-shaped mushrooms. What had her father said, long ago? "The white ones that grow on stumps are . . ." She could not remember. But they were, he had said, good to eat. How to be sure these were the same? She pulled her blanket around her, stepping softly, skirting the chipmunk, and walked barefoot into the rain.

They *looked* the same. She broke off a crumb and tasted it . . . "oyster" . . . That was the name—"oyster mushrooms." They had a faint oysterish taste, but they were really more like meat, or like meat and bread mixed. She broke off another piece. It was delicious. She knew that some mushrooms tasted all right but were nonetheless poisonous. Still, the chipmunk was eating them. Could they poison people and not chipmunks? She doubted it. She picked a double handful and took them back to the hollow. As night fell, she ate them all, and went back to sleep feeling warm, full, and reasonably content.

The next day her walking improved, and so did the weather. Though it stayed cloudy and chilly, the rain stopped, and the ground dried out underfoot. She limped along quite nimbly all morning, though without the sun to guide her she still had to stay within sight of the crevasse. She had taken with her enough mushrooms to last the day—in fact, she had taken them all, except a few she left for the chipmunk.

Early in the afternoon, something began happening to the crevasse. With each few hundred feet she progressed, it grew narrower, until, except for her ankle, she could easily have jumped across. She went to the edge, lay down, and peered into it. As far as she could tell, it was still as deep as ever, and she was quite sure she could see the brook still running below, now covering the whole bottom.

She walked on, keeping closer than ever to the edge, since now she could scarcely see it at all. And then it disappeared entirely. The edges simply met, like the end of a long piece of pie; and from there on, the trees grew right across it. She walked back to the last bit where a crack was still visible and stared down again. She could see nothing but blackness. The brook continued somewhere down there in a tunnel of its own. But she had lost her guideline.

For the next few hundred yards or so she could continue in the direction the crevasse had been running. After that, when it was out of sight for good, there would be no way to tell which way she was going. People who walk in the woods with nothing to guide them, she had read, always ended up walking in great circles, getting nowhere.

But as it turned out she need not have worried. For she had hardly gone out of sight of the crevasse when she came, abruptly, to the end of her journey.

The castle rose before her like a black thundercloud. There was the high fence, just as Otto had described it, enclosing a grassy courtyard as big as a village. Through it, crosscrossing it like a gridiron, ran the strange black paths, shiny as wet asphalt, but curiously metallic in appearance. And just as Ellen arrived, a group of people came walking down one of them, heading toward her.

As they came closer, she saw that they were all boys, dressed in black. There were perhaps 50 of them, marching four abreast, not in step but in a sort of pathetic, shuffling disorder. They were all very careful to stay on the path, however.

Then, as they came directly in front of her and the column began to turn to her right, she saw that the boy nearest her in the second row was Otto. As he turned, his eyes looked directly into hers, but they were as blank as the eyes of a sheep.

Elementary Destruction

IT had been Ellen's intention to walk as far as the castle, determine where it was and perhaps find out, if she could, whether Otto was there as she had suspected. She had not planned to enter it, nor even go very near it. Instead, she would continue the journey over the pass, find Aunt Sarah, and together they would figure out what to do about Otto.

But the expression on his face! What had they done to him? He had been so lively and smart, his face quick to brighten and change, his eyes inquisitive and alert. Now he looked . . . Ellen recalled what he had said: ". . . like dead people." That was how he looked. She could not bring herself just to walk away—not quite yet, anyway.

Undecided, she walked along in the edge of the woods, skirting the fence, in the direction the column of boys had gone. She wanted to look at Otto again. She followed them until they disappeared from sight around the front of the castle. Where were they going? She kept on, hoping to see, until she had gone the length of the courtyard. Now she found herself, still in the woods, in front of the castle.

From the front, however, she could not see into the grounds at all. She now understood how the place was laid out. The great courtyard around the castle was precisely square. Three sides of the square were guarded by the high fence with the barbed wire on top. The fourth, the front, had a wall of solid stone. It was just as high as the fence, and from where she stood it hid all but the highest of the castle's towers. The castle itself stood toward the front of the courtyard, closer to the wall than to the fences.

She examined the wall. In the exact center, a couple of hundred yards from where she stood, there was a black iron gate, and it was closed. A gravel driveway led from it and disappeared into the woods. She wondered, briefly, where it led, and then she stopped wondering because the gate itself suddenly cracked in the middle and swung open.

Two men, one to each half, were pushing it, and Ellen recognized their costumes—both were in black, with a green stripe on each leg. When the gate was fully opened, a car drove out. Ellen was startled. It had not occurred to her that there could be so modern—so ordinary—a thing as a car connected with this sinister dark castle. Actually, it was not an ordinary car; it was a big, lumbering vehicle, half bus, half truck, with double wheels on the back and rough tires. It rumbled out of the courtyard and stopped; one of the men who had pushed the gate climbed in beside the driver, and they roared off down the gravel road into the woods. The other man went back inside and pulled the gate shut behind him, one-half at a time.

Now Ellen was more curious than ever as to where the driveway went. She listened for the noise of the engine, but it quickly died away, muffled by the thickness of the forest.

There was no one in sight, and no sound from inside. Half an hour passed. She worked her way along the edge of the woods until she was directly opposite the gate. From here she could see that the two halves did not quite meet in the middle—there was a visible crack between them. She wanted to look through this crack.

To do this she would have to leave the shelter of the woods and walk out in the open—the gate was about two hundred feet from where she stood. Should she risk it? Would she be seen? Was there a lookout somewhere along the wall? She examined it carefully. There was nothing that looked like a peephole, nor anything resembling a sentry box along the top.

She darted out of the woods, and a moment later she was peering through the crack with one eye. Inside she could see part, but not all, of the front of the castle. The gravel drive on which she stood led to a massive front door, framed by dark pillars. But once inside the wall, the driveway was no longer gray gravel; it turned black, the same shiny black as the paths she had seen earlier.

About halfway up the largest of the castle towers, on the front side, she saw a large, multi-faceted bay window. It was the only real glass window in the castle; the others, where there were any, were merely dark slits. She stared at this window and thought she could see someone moving behind it, looking out, but she could not be sure.

Then something else caught her eye. In front of the gate —directly under the bay window but partly out of her field of vision—stood a strange, square enclosure like a very large playpen. Its sides were of open fencework, waist high. Its floor, what she could see of it through the crack, looked as if it were made of heavy black close-knit wire screen. There was a man pacing in this playpen thing, disappearing from her view and then reappearing. He held his head in his hands as if it were aching.

She did not hear the car coming until it was nearly upon her. But someone inside had been listening, or knew somehow, for she saw a black-clad figure run to the gate —run to within six inches of her intent eye—and as the rumbling engine came out of the woods, the gate swung heavily open. She had no place to hide. She was trapped.

Not quite. The right half of the gate opened first. She jumped aside. Then, as the left half swung toward her, she moved with it. By the time it had opened all the way, she was behind it, between it and the wall. Not much of a hiding place, but it gave her a minute, and she could see out between the hinges. She scrunched herself as small as she could and waited. The car was the same one she had seen before.

But it had picked up some passengers. It stopped just inside the gate, almost in front of her nose. The back opened and five—no, six—children got out. Five boys first, and then, lagging, a girl about a year older than Ellen. They were not dressed in black, but in ragged clothing.

Two men in black uniforms watched the children as they climbed out of the bus. Each child, as he stepped down onto the black path, stood stock-still and faced the castle, as if awaiting orders. The two men observed this. Then they walked together to the back of the bus to close its heavy door. At this moment, while all backs were turned, Ellen made up her mind. She dashed through the open gate and stood with the other children. A moment later they were all marching toward the castle door, and the iron gate clanged shut behind them. Neither of the two men noticed that there were now seven children instead of six. And none of the children said a word.

The front door opened as they approached it, and they walked through in silence. The two men dropped back as the door closed.

Inside, they stood in a circular antechamber, low-ceilinged, black-floored, dimly lit with weak, flickery electric light bulbs. It was not at all like the arched, gay, gold-and-stained-glass entrance hall Ellen had once dreamed in her own castle. But she did not have much time for comparisons. Six long corridors led off like the arms of a starfish from the room they stood in, and without a second's hesitation the children walked off down one of them.

How did they know where they were supposed to go? Had they been here before? Ellen did not think so. They moved almost as if they were getting silent orders from somewhere. If so, Ellen was not getting them. She followed the others down the hall.

Now that she was inside, she wondered why she had done it. It was to rescue Otto, of course, she told herself.

But she had not even the slightest idea where to find Otto in this vast, dark building. And if she did find him, she did not believe for a minute that they would let her just take him and walk out. And who were *they*, anyway? And what was the whole place *for?* Why were all these children here, and what did they do? And she realized that it was curiosity, almost as much as wanting to help Otto, that had made up her mind so suddenly. It had probably been a foolish thing to do.

But it was done; she was inside. For the moment, at least, her best plan would be to stay with the other children. Obviously they were supposed to be here, and she was not. If she did what they did, perhaps she would not be noticed. She would play for time, and learn what she could learn.

As they walked down the corridor they passed doors, all closed. At first she thought the castle was filled with nothing but mysterious, absolute, overwhelming silence. But now, from behind some of these doors, she heard noises. From one of them, a busy hammering. From another, voices—children's voices—chanting in unison. It sounded like school.

Her small group stopped at one of the doors and went in. It was a Quartermaster's Depot. Behind a table sat a young man in black (but no green stripes), and behind him stood shelves of clothing. The children fell into line, and Ellen sprang in at the rear. She wished they did not know quite so quickly what to do. Even more she wished that somebody would say something—even just, "Hey, you."

There was a portion of the wall marked with feet and

inches, upward and sideward. The first boy stood in front of it, snapped erect, marched to the Quartermaster, and received a small stack of clothes. The second followed. The feet and inches told the size; the young man had only to glance, and reach behind him.

It was Ellen's turn. She stood erect in front of the wall as the others had done, braced for sudden and disastrous discovery, ready to run. The young man was going to say: "There were only supposed to be six. Who are you?" But he did not, and in a moment she, too, had a uniform. There were closets the size of phone booths to change in. She changed in frantic haste, so she would be ready when the others were. The black uniform was rather scratchy, but fit well enough. There was no difference between the boys' and the girls' suits: black slacks with an elastic waist, and a black pullover shirt.

What should she do with her own clothes? With her rucksack? Leave them in the closet. But she took out her handbag and slipped it on her wrist. Could she keep it? Did anybody here carry a handbag? No. She found a pocket in her uniform, slipped her $1.21 and her letter into it, and tucked the handbag into the rucksack. She was ready.

So were the other six, all in black uniforms like her own. Back out into the hall, again without a word, and through another door. A dining room! A somber room as big as a theater, and almost as dim, with endless rows of long wooden tables and benches, all empty now. Obviously it was past the regular eating hour, but they were to be fed anyway. There was soup, bread, cheese, milk (canned); there were knives, spoons, trays and bowls,

along a cafeteria counter—again, it reminded Ellen of a
school, only dingier. But she was grateful for the food.
They served themselves, and since no one seemed to no-
tice, she heaped her tray with bread and filled her glass
and soup bowl level full. It was tasteless food, but Ellen
wolfed it down as if she were starving, as, in fact, she very
nearly was.

After lunch the trouble began. When they had stood up
from eating and dumped their trays into a tub of grimy
dishwater, the children went back into the hall—but this
time they separated, and headed in different directions.
Three of the boys vanished abruptly through a door, two
others walked one way down the hall; the girl walked the
other way. Ellen, in a panic of indecision, looked one way,
then the other as they left her. Then she ran and caught
up with the girl. Perhaps girls were supposed to stay together.

The girl went the whole length of the corridor, turned
left into another, and stopped in front of a door. She
seemed unaware that Ellen was following her. She opened
the door, and they went in.

It was a classroom they had entered. It looked like a
lot of other classrooms Ellen had been in before, only it
had no windows. Still it was more brightly lit than the
dark corridors or the dining room, and, for a wonder, people were talking. The girl went directly to an empty desk
and sat down. Ellen sat in the empty desk behind her.
About a third of the desks—there were some thirty in all
—were empty. In the front of the room, facing the children, stood the teacher, a man dressed in black with the
familiar green stripes. These must be, Ellen decided, a

sign of rank or authority. In the front row a boy was reading aloud from a book. All the others were listening to him and following in their own books. So was the teacher.

There was a book on the desk in front of Ellen. It had a cardboard cover, on which was printed the title:

Elementary Destruction
Second-Grade Readings in Destructive Behavior

What a strange title for a lesson book. Then Ellen saw something stranger still. In the lower right hand corner of the cover there was a picture, an imprimatur, of a crown exactly the same shape as her crown, but jet black. Under the crown, in small print, was the word "Hieronymus." The name rang in Ellen's mind like a minor chord.

She saw that the girl ahead of her had opened her book to page 13, and also that the boy who had been reading had stopped. The class looked at the teacher. He turned the page in his book, pointed it at another boy, and said:

"You, 729B—read page fourteen."

729B, a thin boy with yellow hair—Ellen could see only the back of his head—began to read.

The Dungeon

THE boy's voice read:

Aesop's Fables: The Smart Little Horsefly

Once there was a smart horsefly. He had a very sharp bite. He liked to bite horses and make them jump. The fly was so quick and clever that the horses could never catch him.

"That's not like any Aesop's fable *I* ever read," thought Ellen, following in her book.

The horsefly hated people even worse than horses. He hated nice, happy people most of all. One day Mr. Brown, Mrs. Brown and their four jolly children went on a picnic. The little horsefly hid in the car. He hid under the seat. Soon they were speeding along the highway at 60 miles an hour. Then the little horsefly zipped out from under the seat. He bit Mr. Brown first on one eye, then on the other.

"Oh!" cried Mr. Brown. "Oh! Oh! Look! Look! Look! I cannot see!"

The little horsefly laughed and flew out the window. Mr.

Brown could not steer the car. He drove into the wrong lane. His car hit three other cars—crash! crash! crash! Mr. Brown and Mrs. Brown were killed. So were their four jolly children and eighteen other nice, happy people.

Moral: A *little* damage at the right time and place does a *lot* of damage.

Ellen thought: "That's *terrible*. That's the worst fable I ever heard." She felt like shouting it.

She looked at the other pages in her book. On each page there was a story or a rhyme, but all were horribly twisted or distorted. On page 1 she read:

> Mary had a little lamb
> Its fleece was white as snow,
> And everywhere that Mary went
> The lamb was sure to go.

"So far, so good," she thought. But then:

> It followed her to school one day
> Which was against the rule
> It bit the teacher on the leg
> And knocked her off the stool.

"That's *wrong*."

> "Hit the teacher! Hit the teacher!"
> All the children cried.
> And each of them picked up a rock
> And stoned her till she died.

Ellen was aghast. What kind of lessons were these? What kind of horrible school?

But 729B had now finished reading about Mr. Brown and the horsefly, and the teacher spoke again.

"You," he said, "751B. Read page fifteen."

He was a small boy with dark hair, in the far corner of

the room. From where she sat Ellen could hardly see him. She glanced at the title on page fifteen:

"Peter Pan:
A Brave Boy Who Hated Grownups"

Peter Pan was one of her favorite stories. She shuddered to hear how it would turn out in this awful book.

Then the boy began to read aloud. The voice was Otto's.

Ellen leaped for joy at the sound. She had found him! Without thinking, she sprang out of her seat. Her book fell to the floor with a thump. She banged against her desk and the whole thing, desk, chair and all, went crashing over. Ellen stood beside them in dismay. The teacher looked at her with cold, dark eyes. He walked over to her, as all the children stared. He stood before her.

"I think," he said, "that you are out of tune."

Ellen had no idea what "out of tune" meant. Still, she must deny it.

"Oh, no, sir," she said. "I slipped, that's all." She could not look at him, but tried to right the fallen desk. She was trembling.

"Furthermore," he said, "I don't seem to have a number for you."

"No, sir," she began. "I just got here. There hasn't been time . . ."

The teacher spoke sharply to the new girl in front of Ellen.

"What is your number?"

The girl answered without hesitation:

"My number is 22G."

"Correct," said the teacher.

Ellen tried to cover up.

"Mine is 23G," she said. "I came in just behind her."

The teacher went to his desk and checked in a book that lay on it.

"There *is* no 23G," he said. He pushed a button on the wall behind his desk.

The jig was up.

Within seconds—or so it seemed to Ellen—two heavy-shouldered, muscular teen-age boys hurried into the room, looking this way and that like hunting dogs. Ellen was still standing. The teacher pointed his chin at her and nodded. Without a word they gripped her, one to each elbow (though not roughly), and led her away. As she left, she thought of something. She was caught. What could she lose?

"That is *not* an Aesop's fable," she said, addressing not the teacher but the other children. "They just made it up. It's not real."

They stared at her with blank eyes. Except that in the other corner of the room she thought she saw Otto give a faint smile of recognition.

The two boys steered her from the room, down the corridor, through a door, down a stairs, down another corridor to another stairs. This one was a narrow, dark, spiral stairway, like a corkscrew in a bottomless well, plunging deep into the rocky earth beneath the castle. They made three complete turns down the spiral and stopped at a circular landing surrounded by doors. Ahead of them the stairs led down still deeper, into blackness, but they chose one of the doors instead. Another corridor, smaller, narrower, arch-ceilinged, so dark Ellen had to peer to see where she was going. An iron door with a small, square, barred window. They produced a key, unlocked the door, pushed her inside, locked it, and walked away, their footsteps rattling off into the distance like echoes in an empty subway. Ellen was alone.

The room she stood in was so dark that at first she could not tell how big it was; she stood still inside the door, not daring to move for fear of bumping into something. Slowly her eyes adjusted, and in a few minutes she saw four walls, three of rough concrete, the other—the rear wall—of natural stone. She had furniture: a bed with a stiff straw mattress and one blanket, a straight wooden chair. The room was five paces from front to back, six paces from side to side. The only door was the iron one she had entered. It was a cell. She was in a dungeon. She was a prisoner. And so far she had learned only one useful thing. Otto was number 751B, whatever that meant.

She sat on the edge of the bed. She had, she now realized, got herself into a dreadful mess. She was locked up and helpless, and it was her own fault. Meanwhile Otto, apparently equally helpless, was upstairs being taught the most sickening lies. It suddenly dawned on her: they were teaching those children to be *evil*. They were teaching that bad was good and good was bad. But why? What was the purpose?

And why, *why* had she not had the sense to get away, to leave while she was still free? Surely if she and Aunt Sarah went to the police, they would arrest the people who ran this place. They had no right to lock her up like this. Or had they? After all, it was she who had trespassed; it was their place; they could claim they thought she was a thief. But she wasn't—not that it made any difference, since they didn't have to claim anything to anybody. They had her. And all she had wanted was to help Otto.

The more she thought about it, the more indignant she got. Gradually, the fear she had felt gave way to anger. Somehow or other, she was going to get out of here—and get Otto out, too.

What one is supposed to do when locked in a cell, she recalled, is to inspect every square inch of the walls, ceiling and floor, and find a loose brick, a sliding panel, or a cleverly concealed tunnel dug by some unknown earlier occupant. Or listen for a faint tapping on the wall, a signal from another prisoner who is ready to escape.

She started her inspection immediately, and to her own surprise she did discover two things—neither of them, however, likely to be of much help in escaping. One was that the side walls of the room did not reach quite all the way to the ceiling. She could not tell just how wide a gap there was, because it was too high up—far higher, alas, than she could jump or climb. But there was definitely a gap on each side, probably, she guessed, for ventilation, and through one of these came part of the light that kept her cell from being completely dark. It was a faint glow—as if, perhaps, there was a light in the next room and she was getting a reflection from it.

This illumination, plus a feeble glow that filtered in through the barred window in her door, was all the light her room had. Considering this, it was surprising that she could see at all. The rear wall was the reason: it was made chiefly of jet-black stone, but mixed with it here and there were patches of the same sparkling material she had seen in the walls of the cave. Even in this dim light it glowed faintly. And when she examined the wall inch-by-inch she realized that it was not a man-made wall; there were no seams, no blocks. It was solid. How had they ever cut through it to shape these rooms and these long corridors?

Then she heard a faint tapping.

It was on the door, not on the wall—a timid, breathless kind of knock. A trick! Just the way an executioner would knock so you would not be forewarned when you opened the door and saw the hooded figure with the sharp, curve-bladed axe. Ellen crouched behind the chair. They would not fool her. The knock came again.

But when the voice spoke, it was the voice of a girl.

"Can I come in?"

"Who are you?"

"Genevieve. I'm from the next room."

Ellen left her crouch and looked through the bars. On the other side was the thin, pale face of a girl with light blue eyes. Her hair hung, wispy and unhealthy, around her shoulders.

Ellen said, "I can't open the door. It's locked."

"I can. I have a key."

A key! Who was this girl? Ellen turned crafty. She waited just inside the door.

"Open it."

"I can't unless you promise to stay in."

"Why not?"

"They told me not to."

So she was one of them.

"What do you want?"

"Nothing. Just to talk."

"Okay. Come on in."

"You won't try to come out?"

"No." What could she lose? If the girl didn't open the door, she could certainly not get out.

The lock clicked, the door opened, and the girl entered. "Anyway," she said, "it wouldn't do any good. There's a bigger door at the end of the hall, and it's locked, too."

She was the thinnest, palest, sickliest, saddest-looking girl Ellen had ever seen. She was older than Ellen—perhaps fourteen. She sat on the edge of the wooden chair.

"You live in the room next door?" Ellen asked, greatly puzzled.

"Yes. What's your name?"

"Ellen. But what are you? A prisoner?"

"Sort of. I'm a trusty."

"What's that?"

"It means I can have a key, and I help with some of the work, but I can't go upstairs. Except when they send for me. I'll be bringing you your meals, I expect. And I'll show you where the bathroom is. It's down the hall."

"But why are you down here? What did you do?"

"I'm out of tune. You must be, too."

"That's what that man said—a teacher. What's it mean?"

"You don't know?"

"I don't know anything. I just got here."

"It means the machine doesn't work on you."

"What machine?"

"The machine in the tower. The Hieronymus Machine."

There was that name again.

"Who is Hieronymus?"

"The king."

"King of what?"

Genevieve's face grew cloudy. "King of . . . I don't know exactly. He's just the king."

"He must be king *of* someplace."

"I don't know."

"Anyway, I didn't see any machine."

"Oh, you don't see it." She leaned over and whispered in Ellen's ear. "But I did see it one time."

"What does it do?"

"I don't understand it exactly myself. But it's something like a radio station. Only it doesn't broadcast music and stuff. It broadcasts . . . *feelings.*"

"Feelings? What kind of feelings?"

"All kinds. Any kind the king wants it to. You know those black paths outside?"

"Yes. I mean, I saw them."

"Most people, when they get on those paths, can feel what the machine wants them to do, and they have to do it. They *want* to do it. They're in tune." And she added sadly, "But it doesn't work on me."

"Me either," Ellen said. "I didn't feel a thing."

But that explained how the other children had known so quickly where to go and what to do, and why they had not talked at all. They were hypnotized—it was some kind of a hypnotism machine, or a telepathy machine. Obviously it must work inside the castle, too. She asked Genevieve.

"It works all through the castle," Genevieve said. "It works through some kind of black stuff that's in the stone here. But in the classrooms they can turn it off—or up, or down. The teacher does it."

"I wonder why."

"I think it's because you can't learn things very well when it's turned on. You can't think well enough. I did fine in the classes. But when the class was over and they turned it back on, I never knew what to do. So I have to stay down here."

She added, rather wistfully, "But they think I can learn. I get treatments twice a week. I hope I can."

"You hope you *can?*" Ellen was incredulous. "But it's *awful*. The whole thing is terrible. Why do you want to?"

"Because they'll never let me go outside with the others if I don't. You don't know how sick you get of staying down here."

"How long have you been here?"

"I'm not sure. But more than a year."

A year! No wonder she looked so pale and sick. Ellen leaned over and took Genevieve's hand and spoke very softly.

"Why not just get out altogether? That's what I'm going to do. At least I'm going to try."

But Genevieve had no chance to answer, because just then there came another knock on the door.

The Screen

ELLEN thought, well at least they're polite. They knock before they enter.

"Who is it?" she said.

"May I come in?" It was a man's voice, very friendly.

"That's Brother Michael," whispered Genevieve. "He's nice. He's from the King's tower."

"Come in," said Ellen, dubiously, opening the door. How could he be nice if he worked here?

Yet he was, or at any rate he seemed to be, which is not necessarily the same thing. He was not surprised to see Genevieve in the room.

"Hello, Jenny," he said. Then he turned to Ellen. "I'm Brother Michael. And I don't even know your name."

"Ellen . . ." She started to tell her full name, and then thought better of it. Why should she? "Ellen . . . Jones," she said.

The man had a pleasant smile, though perhaps a bit too

bland and ready, and a round, red, good-natured face.
But the oddest thing was, he was dressed like a monk, in
a black robe with a long skirt that hid his shoes, and even
a medieval bald pate with a fringe of hair cut in a circle
around it. But the rope around his middle was shimmering green, and there were narrow green stripes, like an
admiral's, around the ends of his long black sleeves. He
was part of the organization, all right, despite his kindly
smile.

"Well, Ellen," he said, with a wink, "I hear you don't
think much of our Aesop's Fables."

"No." She did not know whether to be polite or defiant.

"Also, that despite the precautions of two of our best
drivers, you managed to stow away on our bus. They per-
sist in denying that you could have, which is stupid of
them, since after all, here you are."

"Oh, but I . . ." Ellen started to explain, and then
again changed her mind. If they thought she had come on
the bus, let them. The less they knew, the better.

"Don't worry your head about it," said Brother Michael. He chuckled. "You fooled them, and you fooled us.
But we're glad to have you, believe me. We're delighted."

"Why?"

"Well, now," said Brother Michael, becoming just a
shade evasive, "I can't explain everything at once. But put
it this way: some of the hardest-won recruits make the
best soldiers."

"Soldiers?"

"Just my way of speaking. But we are, you see, training
a sort of an army. We're trying to make a soldier out of
Jenny here." He chucked Jenny under the chin. "You

haven't told her much about our plans?"

"No, Sir," said Jenny. "I didn't have time."

"Good!" said Brother Michael. "Then I can tell her as we go. And maybe show her a few things. I'll bet she'd enjoy a look at Advanced Demolition. Eh?"

"Oh, yes, Sir," said Jenny. And to Ellen, "It's very exciting."

Brother Michael looked at his watch. "They should be starting the Arson Lesson in ten minutes. Let's go."

Ellen said warily, "Where are we going?"

"To the tower. But we can take a quick look at a few things on the way."

Ellen did not want to go. She did not trust anyone here, including Jenny and Brother Michael. And what awaited her in the tower?

But she did not want to stay here, either. If she was to escape from this place and rescue Otto, she had to learn her way around it. So when Brother Michael opened the door, she went out, and followed him nervously down the hall.

Five or six corridors and several flights of stairs later, they paused outside a door. From the other side came the thud of an explosion.

"Ah, just in time," said Brother Michael, who was breathing hard from the walk. He rang a bell before entering, a wise precaution, judging by the noise.

They entered a very large room acrid with smoke. Staring at them, a knot of tall boys in black—they looked fifteen, sixteen and seventeen years old—stood around a gaunt man whose familiar face made Ellen turn immediately and try to run.

She knew him; it was the Stranger.

But the door had closed behind them, and Brother Michael caught her easily by the arm.

"Don't be afraid," he said. "That's Captain Julio. He's one of the most skillful arson teachers we have." And he called out, "Proceed, Captain. We're not here to interrupt —merely to observe." He whispered to Ellen, "I know he looks fearful, but he won't hurt you."

Captain Julio scarcely glanced at Ellen. He turned back to his work, and Ellen realized to her relief that he did not recognize her. Of course! He had never actually seen either her or Otto.

The boys watched while the Captain filled a bottle, an ordinary green ginger ale bottle, with clear fluid from a metal tank. At the far end of the room, which was as big as a basketball court, stood a mock-up of a brick house. That is, there was the front of a house, but no back or sides and no roof. There were empty windows and a gaping doorway.

The captain handed the filled bottle to one of the boys. The boy set the bottle instantly and efficiently between his feet, ripped a strip of cloth from a sheet lying on the floor, and rolled the cloth into a plug. Upending the bottle, he applied a match, then hurled the fiery missile, flame forward, spinning like a football, at the house. A Molotov cocktail. It arched neatly through the lower right front window. There came a *thrump* of explosion, and flames billowed gorgeously out all the windows and the door. Ellen had to admit—in a gruesome way, it was exciting.

"Beautiful!" said Brother Michael loudly.

Captain Julio gave him a glare of pure contempt and

filled the next bottle. "He's not very friendly," whispered Brother Michael, steering Ellen out the door, "but results count. Every boy in that group is ready for Chicago next week."

"What will they do in Chicago?"

Brother Michael looked at her reproachfully. "You haven't been reading the newspapers this summer."

"No." That was true.

"More than 300 killed so far, and there isn't a decent citizen in the city who will stick his head out after dark. Eight million dollars damage! And our boys are doing it. Not alone, of course. But ours are *trained;* they teach the others."

"You mean race riots?"

"Race riots. Juvenile gangfights. Rumbles. Motorcycle rallies. Looting. Fires. Bombs. Snipers. Whatever it is, we're there. And the police! They lock the doors of their squad cars, and they don't get out. Our Kill-the-Cop Course is the best series we have—naturally, since the King teaches it personally. I don't mean just methodology! I mean motivationally, too. When our boys see a uniform . . . Well, it's remarkable. Especially when you consider that they learn entirely on dummies."

"On dummies!" Ellen exclaimed, struck by a memory.

"Well, it's hard to get real policemen to practice on."

"I can imagine." In the past ninety seconds it had dawned on Ellen that nice though he might seem, Brother Michael was quite mad. They were walking along a corridor again, and he took another look at his watch.

"We have time for just a *look* at the crafts department before we go to the tower. I've got to get you back to your room in time for supper."

He opened another door. This was a trade-school class, a workshop. Boys were hammering, cutting pipes with hacksaws, planing wood, boring holes, grinding metal with whirring Carborundum stones. It looked, at first, *sane*. Then she saw that the end product was, in every case, a deadly weapon of some sort. Homemade knives with long, vicious blades, homemade bombs of tamped pipes, heavy blunt pistols with pipe barrels. "Not very satisfactory," murmured Brother Michael, "but better than nothing. There's all this talk about restricting firearms, you know. We have to be ready. But look at this."

Two boys were at work with chisels, drills, sandpaper, on yard-long stalks of hollow bamboo. To these they were fitting little tufted darts tipped with needle-points.

"An experiment," said Brother Michael. "A little idea of my own. Blowguns. They're quiet, cheap, easy to make. In the chemistry shop, just down the hall here, they're getting to work on curare. Other kinds of venom, too, of course. Black widow has great possibilities. I know it's pretty far out, but you never know till you try."

"It doesn't seem so far out to me," Ellen said, playing along, and Brother Michael was tremendously pleased.

"You don't think so? Would you like to volunteer for blowgun training? I could arrange it. You'd be the first girl in Weapons. We're just starting with girls, you know." He sighed. "But I guess that's premature. We've got to get you in tune first. We'd better go on."

As they went on, Ellen ventured one question. It had been puzzling her since she first entered the castle: "Where do all the children come from?"

"Our recruits? Ah, now you're asking secrets. But I'll give you a hint: it's amazing—deplorable, really—how careless people are about children. A school burns down, a school bus wrecks, an orphanage blows up. 'Thirty-six Killed,' the headlines say. But were there really 36 killed? Or were there perhaps only 30 killed and 6 they just couldn't find? 'Five Missing,' the newspaper says. Do you know what 'missing' means? It means we've got five new recruits! How many children disappear in a year from a Harlem tenement block? Take my word for it—recruits are not hard to come by. Competent teachers, now, are something else again, but I won't go into that."

So, Ellen thought, these were all just ordinary children who had had the bad luck to fall into the wrong hands. Or was it bad luck? She had a horrible thought. A school burns down, Brother Michael had said, or an orphanage blows up. She thought of the Advanced Demolition class. Could it be . . . ? She did not dare ask.

In any case, there wasn't time. They had entered one last corridor, which broadened as they walked and led into an abrupt change of atmosphere. They had reached the outside of a large octagon: the tower. You could only see four sides as you approached, of course, and one of these framed a door of brilliant green. It had no door-knob, but a panel of gold-colored translucent material. Brother Michael laid his right hand against this panel and the door swung open.

The octagonal room they entered was, by contrast with the outer drabness, gorgeous. It was plush; it strove for elegance, but did not quite achieve it. The thick green carpet had come from a mail-order catalogue: "Good

Carpeting. Better Carpeting. Our Finest Carpeting."
Ellen's feet sank deep into it as they walked across the
huge room to a shiny brass sliding door: an automatic
elevator.

They got off at the third floor. Somewhere above, Ellen
realized, must be the tower room with all the bay windows. This room, however, had no windows at all. It had,
rather, glass-walled cubicles off a center room into which
they had stepped from the elevator. They entered one of
these, and Ellen quickly learned she had been tricked. She
should not have trusted Brother Michael: the instant they
were both inside, he stepped quickly out and clicked the
glass door shut behind him. There was no handle, no
knob, nor any way to open it. She was trapped.

She looked around her. Three walls of the cubicle were
glass—but heavy, thick glass, not the kind you can break
without a sledge-hammer. The fourth was the stone wall
of the tower itself. A wooden chair stood in the corner.
Then she noticed the floor. It was woven of wire screen,
like the playpen thing she had seen outside. The wire was
shiny black, as heavy as a cattle fence, but much more
closely knit.

She watched Brother Michael through the glass. On the
other side of the main room he stood at a panel set with
dials and knobs, like a very complicated radio. There was
also an intercom. A speaker clicked on in the ceiling over
her head, and she heard his voice:

"Ellen."

"Yes."

"I'm sorry to trick you. But I thought you might not
want to go in if I told you."

"What are you going to do?"

"Nothing that hurts. You're going to get a treatment—like Genevieve. We want to get you in tune."

"But I don't want to get in tune."

"I know. That's why I tricked you."

He flicked a switch on the panel, set two knobs, turned another one just a fraction. A needle on a white dial flickered a shade. (From zero to one? She could not read the figures.) She watched apprehensively. Would she feel something? She braced herself for an electric shock.

"There's a chair," the speaker said in its tin voice, "if you want to sit down."

She stood. Nothing happened. Nothing at all. Brother Michael put on a thing with earphones, a headset, turned the knob a fraction farther, took the headset off again. The needle flickered higher. Still nothing.

His voice again: "There's a chair if you want to sit down." Ellen remained standing, staring through the glass.

This ritual, including the reminder about the chair, was repeated five times. The needle moved farther across the dial each time, like the speedometer of a car spurting faster and faster, until, on the fifth try, it moved all the way across. Ellen felt exactly as she had before, except that her apprehension was disappearing. She knew, somehow, that whatever Brother Michael was doing, it wasn't going to work. She watched him with calm eyes. She saw that he was sweating.

There was a click, and a strange voice broke in on the intercom.

"Brother Michael, may we assume that it is you?"

Brother Michael's voice said, "Yes, Sir."

"The King does not appreciate your draining the circuits during the exercise period. Already three subjects have strayed off the malignite paths."

"I apologize, Sir. I was treating a patient."

"Surely not with Alpha Force 20."

"Yes, Sir. The patient shows no response."

"No response? At Force 20?"

A pause.

"Please repeat what you just reported."

"I have treated the patient at standard angles 33 and 66 degrees, standard frequency 4,000 cycles, at Alpha forces from one to twenty. The patient shows no reaction of any kind."

A click. A longer pause. Another click.

"Is the patient male or female?"

"Female. It's the girl who stowed away on the bus."

"Please return her to her room and observe all precautions. The King will speak to her in person tomorrow morning."

A Way Out

"E LLEN?" said Jenny that night. "Can you hear me?"

The voice came over the wall, through the gap. Ellen was alone in her room, sitting on the edge of her cot. She had eaten dinner from a tray someone had shoved through the door.

"Yes. Come on in."

"I can't. They took my key away. I'm locked in."

"Why?"

"I don't know. I thought it must be because of you. Did you do something . . . bad?"

"I didn't do anything at all. That man—Brother Michael—showed me some of the classes. Then he put me in a glass room with a wire floor."

"That's the screen."

"What's it for?"

"That's where they put me for treatments. It's connected to the machine."

"The Hieronymus Machine?"

"Yes. The hypnotism is much stronger in there. When I'm in there, I can get in tune. That's what the treatments are for. If you can get in tune often enough and long enough, you stay in tune. At least, that works with most people."

Brainwashing, Ellen thought. She said:

"When you're 'in tune' do you . . . *know* things? Do they teach you things? About this place?"

"Oh, yes. You know everything about it. You know what to do, and why, and you know it's good."

"Do you know what 751 B is?"

"That's somebody's number. They use numbers instead of names because it's more efficient. They're very efficient."

"But what does it *mean?* Does it tell who it is? Or where?"

" 'B' means it's a boy. The number would tell something about how old he is and what group he's in. And what bunk he sleeps in."

"What bunk?"

"In the boy's dormitory."

"Where's that?"

"Upstairs. On the back side of the castle. The side away from the tower."

So that would be where Otto slept—in bunk number 751. A little bit of useful information.

"Ellen?"

"Yes?"

"Remember what you asked me?"

"When?"

"When Brother Michael came in."

"About escaping?"

"Yes. Did you mean it?"

Ellen felt a small stir of excitement.

"Of course I meant it. I'm going to get out, somehow. If they don't . . . kill me or something."

"They won't kill you."

"Then I'm going to escape. Why?"

"I've been thinking about it."

"Thinking what?"

"At first I didn't want to. I thought I was nearly in tune, and that was all I wanted to do—get in tune. But now . . ."

"Yes?"

"Now they've locked me up again. Don't you see? I'm *not* nearly in tune or they wouldn't do that. They wouldn't think they had to."

"Yes, I see."

"I can't stay down here another year. It might be two years. You don't know what it's like." Her voice sounded on the watery edge of tears.

"All right," said Ellen, very confident. "Let's escape. We'll go together." She was pleased, of course. Jenny knew her way around; Jenny knew the ropes.

"But how? When?"

"Look. Can they hear us?"

"Here?"

"Yes. I mean, are there microphones or something?"

"No."

"You're sure?"

"Yes."

"All right. We can start trying now. How big is the gap between the wall and the ceiling?"

"I can't see it well enough to tell."

If only it weren't so *dark*.

"Do you have a light in your room?"

"Yes. It hangs from the ceiling. It's dim, though."

"Stand on your chair and see if you can reach it."

A rattling. A chair dragging. "I can."

"Hold it over as close to the gap as you can." Ellen walked to the far side of her own room and stood on her chair. In a moment the faint glow coming through the gap grew visibly brighter, and the gap itself clearly outlined. It looked horribly narrow—six or seven inches—but just possibly big enough.

Ellen hopped down.

"Have you got a blanket?"

"Yes."

"Fold it up as small as you can. Bring your chair over near the gap, and see if you can throw it through."

Jenny asked no questions. Two minutes later a blanket like Ellen's own plopped through the gap and fell at her feet. Ellen took both blankets, opened them up, and tied the corner of one to the corner of the other, using a double knot and pulling it hard. She stood on her chair.

"Jenny."

"Yes."

"I'm going to throw your blanket back, but it's tied to mine. You hold down your end—put the bed on it and sit on the bed. I'll climb up this side and see if I can get through the gap."

She rolled the blanket and tossed it through, holding

her end.

She waited until she felt it pull taut on the other side.

"Ready?"

"Ready."

Up she went, heavy, clumsily, hand over hand. Otto would have sailed up. Will a girl's head, turned sideways, go through a ventilation duct? It scraped on both sides. Dirt fell in her left eye. She had a cramp in her shoulder. She had to sneeze. Her knees, eventually, her thinnest part, led the way. Jenny saw them from below—then a foot, a shoulder and at last a face, pink with effort.

"I made it." Ellen scrambled down the blanket, which pulled loose and fell on top of her, all in a heap on Jenny's bed. "Not too bad."

Except for the small light bulb hanging from the ceiling, the room was identical to hers.

"But what's the use? We're still locked in."

"I know." Ellen glanced at the opposite wall. There was, as she had hoped, a gap there, too. "Mainly I wanted to see if I could get through. But look—is the next room locked?"

"It didn't used to be. There was no one in it. There's no one but us on this whole floor."

"Maybe it's still not." Ellen rested two minutes.

"Okay," she said. "Give me a boost. Then toss the blanket through and I'll hold it while you pull yourself up. If the door's open, that is."

It was harder this way. Finally they both had to stand on the bed. Then, with Jenny's hands under one foot, on the third try, Ellen got an arm across the top of the wall, scuffled, scraped, pulled her way through, and lowered herself into the dark room. She landed gently on the floor, knees bent to spare her ankles. She was learning.

She went quickly to the door, turned the knob and pulled. It was locked. *No.* She had forgotten. She pushed. It was unlocked. She opened it just a crack, peered out into the empty, dimly lighted corridor, and closed it softly. Her heart was running like an outboard motor. She was scared.

"Jenny? It's open. Come on over."

"If I can." The blanket came through a minute later. Ellen held on as Jenny climbed.

But bones change in girls between the ages of ten and fifteen, and thin as she was and squeeze as she might, Jenny could not fit through the gap. She sat on the floor, shaking, after the fifth try. Ellen could hear her crying quietly, trying to muffle it.

"Jenny, don't worry. I wasn't going tonight anyway. I just wanted to explore. When the time comes, we'll figure out some way to get you out."

Ellen waited until the crying stopped; then she said:

"Tell me—did you say we're the only ones on this floor?"

"We were. I think we still are."

"Do they have any guards? I mean at night." It would be night now, probably nine or ten o'clock. Not that you could tell, in this dark, windowless place.

"No. That is, they never used to. They don't need them, you see, except for us, and we're locked in. Everyone else is in tune."

"Are there any other people locked in?"

"I'm not sure. Yes. They were down below."

"Who were they?"

"I don't know. They were . . . secret."

"Well, I'm going out."

"Wait."

"Yes?"

"When you get to the end of the hall, you'll come to the stairway."

"I know."

"You won't be able to go up. There's a big iron door, and it's always locked. But I think you can go down."

"What's down there?"

"I've never been. More halls, I think. More rooms."

Ellen opened the door. "I won't stay long. Keep the blanket up there so I can climb back." She closed the door behind her.

Down the dim and flickering corridor to the end. As Jenny had predicted, the door to the up stairway was locked. Leading down, there was no door. Below her, the spiral stairs wound down into blackness. The steps were of crumbling concrete, and there was a heavy smell of dampness in the air. How far down did they go?

That, at least, she could find out. It was, she realized, the wrong direction for escape; but it was exploration; it was information to be had, and lacking better, she would have it.

She counted the steps as she walked down. Twenty-one made a full circle, and she was on another landing. More corridors led off, and the doors here had been left carelessly ajar. She listened. No sound at all except the echo of her own footsteps. She decided against exploring these hallways—for now at least. They looked, sounded and smelled completely deserted. She continued down. Twenty-one more steps—another landing. Then another, and still one more.

The fourth one down—how deep underground must she be now?—was different. Only one corridor led from this landing, and it was shut off by a heavy gate of iron bars and, directly behind that, a locked door. She pushed and pulled; there was no budging either the gate or the door. The door had a large keyhole, however, to which she applied first one eye and then the other. Seeing only blackness, she tried her ear. She thought she could hear people talking. Could it be possible? A few words only, and she could not catch them, very faint, very far off. She heard another sound, too—the deep, steady throbbing of a big machine, barely audible, somewhere far away in the bowels of the castle.

Ellen stayed, listening at the keyhole, for perhaps ten minutes. Once again she thought she heard a voice—a woman's voice?—but only as a faint murmur. Then only silence, silence and the beating of the machine. No doubt whoever had been talking had gone to sleep; it must be very late, close to midnight by now. It was interesting to think about, however; since there was talking, there must be more than one person in that heavily barred corridor. Unless, of course, as sometimes happens, a lonely prisoner had taken to talking to himself. No, *her*self. Then it dawned on her; the first voice, she was quite sure, had not been a woman's, but a man's. Or had it? She could not really remember. It was almost unthinkable that anyone, man or woman, was locked up down here, so deep underground, so far from daylight. It made her own dark cell seem like a sunny attic room.

She continued downward. On the next two descending spirals the light, already almost imperceptible, grew steadily weaker, and in the end she was groping ahead in total darkness so thick it felt like a black mask over her eyes.

Then she was at the bottom. She could see nothing, but the grit of the concrete underfoot gave way to the ring of solid rock. She put her hand down: smooth, cool stone, *damp* stone. Holding her hands straight out, she walked slowly forward. She did not dare go far for fear of losing her sense of direction. She did not know how big a place she was in, and if she wandered away from the stairway, she might never find it again.

I'll take three steps straight ahead, she thought, and then three steps backward, and I'll be where I started. The throb of the machine was slightly louder down here, and mixed with it was a soft, whispering sound like wind blowing, but there was no wind. She took her three steps and her outstretched hand touched a wall: stone, dripping wet. Simultaneously she felt a coldness on her feet. She was standing ankle-deep in water.

She put her hands down again. The water was flowing. She was in a stream—three, possibly four feet wide. It was cool but not icy, and its flow produced the sighing, windlike whisper she had heard. It also probably explained the throb of the machine: this must be where the castle got its water supply; the throb was a pump.

She took her three steps backward, moved back toward the stairs, found them, and sat down. This, then, might be an escape route. If there was a pump somewhere else in this black underground place, then there must be other sections, other stairways, other corridors. But how to find them? It would be virtually impossible to explore down here without a light. She remembered and longed for the matches she had left in her rucksack. They were gone now. But matches, candles, a lantern, even a flashlight should not be impossible to find somewhere in the castle. Jenny might know where to find one or the other; she herself had seen matches in that awful arson class. All right, she thought, I'll sign up for arson and steal some matches.

Meanwhile, there was nothing to do but go back upstairs. Or was there? She had a vague feeling there was. The ghost of an idea lurked around the fringes of her mind, just out of reach. Something she had seen, or heard, or done, or read, or been. As she felt her way up the black stairwell it followed just behind her. She stopped again at the big iron gate, but there were no more voices. Even the machine had stopped pumping. All she could hear was her own hard breathing and her shuffling footsteps, which grew slower and wearier as she climbed her way back up the remaining 84 steps to her own dungeon.

Jenny said, "Did you find anything?"

Ellen said, "I don't know. I'll tell you tomorrow." She fell in total exhaustion on her hard straw mattress, and in seconds, flat on her back, was sound asleep.

But sleep did not drive away the ghost. In Ellen's dreaming mind it grew clearer and bolder. By magic, it split into two ghosts. One was only a voice, calling her from behind an iron gate. It called her name, sadly, over and over again. It was a woman's voice, a voice she knew, but whose or from where she could not remember. But she knew it was the same voice she had heard in the deep dungeon below.

The other ghost was the shade of Ellen herself, walking in a stream of water. She watched herself wade through a pitchblack cave under a mountain, guided only by her feet in the water. The sight excited her. She knew where to go: keep moving *upstream*, she told herself; feel the water flowing backward over your feet. Her ghost kept on obediently, one groping step at a time. Somehow she could see it despite the dark.

Then a joyful thing happened. The blackness was pierced, up ahead, by a broomhandle of light. The ghost waded faster, half running now. She looked up: there, overhead, was a patch of blue sky, and all at once everything looked familiar. There was the pile of boulders. There, on her right, was the cave where her crown was buried. Inside the cave sat Otto, cross-legged, joyfully hammering on a block of wood. He was carving a dove.

The hammering got louder, and Ellen woke up. It was someone knocking on her door. But as she awoke the dream was still vivid in her head, and she knew what it had told her. Of *course*, the stream beneath the castle was the same one that ran at the bottom of the crevasse. It had to be. She need only follow it and it would lead her out, out of the black abyssal dungeons, into the free air.

The knocking kept on. "Come *in*," she said crossly.

The door opened and a portentous voice announced:

"The King will see you now."

It was morning.

Phase 1

$\mathbf{N}$OT two, not three, but four black-clad guards conducted Ellen to the tower. Again she was led into the elevator, but this time it took them to the seventh floor. When it stopped, one of the guards motioned Ellen out the door.

"You will wait here." He stepped back into the elevator with the other three; the silent door closed, and she was alone.

The room in which she stood was small, green in color, and nearly empty. It was windowless, but lit with a subdued green glow which seemed to filter through the ceiling. The only furniture was a green leather chair and a leather-topped table. Set into the table was a button—that is, a round thing like a doorbell-push—and under this a small bronze plaque on which was printed the word:

"Press."

When you see a pushbutton that says "press," your first

instinct is to press it. At least Ellen's was, and she reached out her hand. Then she pulled it back. She sat down in the chair instead. It reminded her of Alice in Wonderland, who was always finding things that said, "Eat me," and eating them, and getting into trouble as a result. How did she know what would happen if she pushed the button? After what she had seen in this place, she would not be surprised if the floor exploded under her feet or the ceiling fell on her head.

No, that was not really likely, since she was in the tower and that was where the King lived. They would not want to wreck it. Still, she was not going to press the button.

She looked around the room more carefully and saw, in the wall opposite where she was seated, a door. She had missed it at first because it was the same color as the wall, and so was the doorknob projecting from it. She got up quickly, walked over and tried it. It was locked.

She sat down again and waited perhaps ten minutes. Then she looked at the button again.

"Press."

They had told her to wait. They had said nothing about pushing a button. Still, the button might be how you let the King know you were waiting. Like a doctor's office— "Ring and Enter." All right.

She jabbed the button with her middle finger.

Instantly there came a *click*, then a faint whirring and a voice spoke. It came from somewhere in the ceiling, and it sounded like a tape or a phonograph record. It was a peculiarly flat, emotionless voice, like a machine speaking, but soft and not unpleasant. It spoke in a meticulously precise English accent.

"The building in which you stand, and the things you have seen in it," said the voice, "are an experiment. You are to become a part of that experiment. Therefore you must learn about it."

The voice paused a moment. Ellen looked at the ceiling, but she could not see any sign of where it came from.

"The experiment is the first part of the Hieronymus Plan. It is called Phase I. It is nearly completed. When Phase I is complete, Phase II will begin."

The voice spoke clearly and simply, and paused after each thought it expressed, as if to give Ellen time to grasp what it said.

"The experiment is run by Hieronymus the King, and by the Hieronymus Machine."

No doubt, thought Ellen, but who was Hieronymus? What was the Hieronymus Machine? Almost as if it read her thoughts, the voice continued.

"Hieronymus is the ancient Latin name that was given to a lonely and scholarly holy man we remember as St. Jerome. He died in the year 420 A.D., at the beginning of the Dark Ages. Some of the followers of St. Jerome formed strange cults, and in the centuries after his death they drifted away from the church. They lived in remote monasteries, often in caves, where they studied the occult, the eldritch, the Forbidden Truths; they developed a science of their own. That science, in later centuries, was almost all lost and forgotten."

Ellen was puzzled. The only science she knew was from her General Science course in the fourth grade. Why were they telling her all this?

"The present experiment is an attempt to re-learn this

ancient science. The Hieronymus Machine itself was first designed and built many centuries ago in a monastery in Spain. It disappeared in the eleventh century, though descriptions of it remained in the ancient writings. An archeologist, digging in a cave near the ruins of the monastery, found it in 1949 and recognized it. The archeologist also found one of the two crowns, also described in the early writings, necessary to make the machine work."

The voice stopped. Then it said:

"To continue your instruction, please press the switch a second time." It clicked dead.

Ellen now began to understand. Two crowns! Could it be that her crown was one of them? Was that why they had locked her up? But no. They had no way of knowing about her crown. She was glad she had followed Mrs. Fitzpatrick's advice and buried it.

Curious, now, she pushed the button again. The voice returned:

"Phase I. This has been a study to learn how effectively the Hieronymus Machine works in conjunction with the black crown. The purpose of the Hieronymus Machine is to change the thoughts and actions of people under its control and to direct them toward the ends for which it was designed."

What does *that* mean? thought Ellen. Blowing up houses? Shooting people with guns?

"The machine exercises control through the use of a black colored mineral called malignite. The black crown is made of pure malignite. The castle and the paths surrounding it are made of a cruder form of malignite, which is found in abundance in the surrounding mountains.

"In Phase I these things have been learned: In the presence of malignite, even in very small quantities, control of human subjects is completely effective in almost one hundred percent of cases. There are a few exceptions."

And I'm one, Ellen thought. And Jenny is another, except she says she does get in tune on that screen. "In tune," of course, must be what they meant by "control."

"Phase I also has studied the effect of a long period of control and training on subjects who are then removed from the influence of the Hieronymus Machine. What happens to a subject who has been controlled for a year, taught to perform certain acts, and is then sent away from the castle to a distant city?"

Like Chicago.

"In almost all cases they continue to do what they have been trained to do. In order to be sure of this, some have been taught to perform disagreeable or even highly dangerous acts—criminal acts, for example, such as attacking armed officers, inciting to riot, or bombing of buildings. We have had no case of disobedience, though we have had a few subjects who forgot both their training and their instructions entirely. Complete loss of memory, it has been learned, is a side effect in certain subjects, but it is infrequent.

"The actions themselves are not important . . ." (Not important? When they kill people?) ". . . except for what they prove: that subjects controlled by the machine continue to follow its orders after they have left it. However, one other important fact has been learned. When subjects follow such orders away from the machine, they tend to perform inefficiently, almost blindly, without regard for consequences. Thus they would be far more efficient if the machine could continue to provide guidance.

"This has led to Phase II, now in its beginning stages."

The voice paused; there was a momentary whirring sound; then it came on again:

"You will now go through the green door directly opposite the table."

How could Ellen go through it when it was locked? But when she tried it again, it had unlocked itself. Ellen opened it and walked into the throne room.

The White-Haired King

S HE noticed three things immediately when she entered the throne room:

A golden door, glowing like sunlight, on the far side of the room.

A black crown, sparkling with evil little red stones.

The King.

The crown was on the King's head, and the King was asleep.

He stared at Ellen as she came in, and he spoke to her, but he was asleep for all that. His eyes were blank glass marbles, and there was no expression in his voice. It was the flat, mechanical voice of the record she had just heard, with the same precise English accent. It said:

"Step forward three paces."

Ellen did as she was told.

"Stop there."

She stopped, perhaps six feet away from the King, who

209

sat in an armchair covered in gold cloth so that it looked *rather* like a throne, but not much.

There was silence while the King stared at her, inch by inch, as if memorizing her for future reference. He looked particularly long into her eyes, and Ellen felt he was trying, through them, to see her thoughts.

Her thoughts were, at the moment, primarily surprise and curiosity, for the King did not look at all as she had expected. Here was no sinister Captain Julio, but an extraordinarily beautiful young man with hair so blond it looked white. He wore no black uniform, but a loose-knit green sweater and tweedy-looking slacks. Young? Perhaps not: with hair that color he could have been twenty-five or sixty-five. In another minute he removed the crown from his head, and then he woke up.

He blinked his eyes, rubbed them, and stared again, as if he had not seen her before. Now his eyes assumed expression, and she noticed they were a lovely shade of blue.

"Come in," he said, though she was already in. "So you're the one that can't be reached." His voice, too, had now lost its flatness, though not its English accent.

"Excuse me?" Ellen did not know what he meant.

"Brother Michael told me all about it. A thorough man, though perhaps a bit simple-minded. Force 20, and no effect at all. Well."

"I don't know what that means."

"We don't either—yet. But I'll tell you this. You're the first to do it. You must have a most unusual mind—and that's what we're interested in."

He stood up, placing the crown carefully on a little jade-topped table beside the throne-chair. Ellen could see that except for the colors, it was an exact duplicate of hers.

The throne room, unlike the other rooms in the tower, had one entire wall of glass—the bay windows she had seen from outside. Thrusting his fists into his pockets, the King walked over to these and stared out. He did not look at all like a king, but rather like a scholar.

"I suppose you're thinking I don't look much like a king." He spoke rather wistfully, and with the faintest of smiles. "You're right, of course. I wasn't cut out for the job. Do you know, I even have ceremonial robes? The title has its uses, of course, in dealing with the lower echelons. But with you I think all that isn't necessary."

He smiled at her with the most charming candor, and Ellen was captivated. And relieved. The King continued:

"I suppose we should get down to business. Did you understand all you heard in the briefing room?"

"Briefing room?"

"The green room you just left."

Ellen thought before answering. "I think I understood it all. Except . . ."

"Except?"

"Except—what's it all *for?* And what does it have to do with me? Why do I have to be part of it? I don't want to."

The King left the window and walked back to Ellen. His blue eyes looked at her gently, and he seemed disappointed and yet very sweet about it, and patient, so that she felt almost sorry for what she had said.

"Of course you don't want to. Not yet. But you don't know enough about it. As you said, you don't know what it's for. You need to see a little bit of . . . what we call Phase II. Meanwhile, I'll tell you this: you are, if you don't mind my saying so, a sort of a monkey wrench."

"I don't understand that, either."

"A small one, perhaps, but you could jam the gears. You don't fit into our Plan. You see, you should have got in tune when you stood on that screen yesterday, and you didn't. Why not? And how many more are there like you?"

"If I don't fit into the plan," Ellen said hopefully, "why don't you just let me go away?"

"I'm afraid we couldn't risk that." The King really sounded regretful. "Not with Phase II almost ready to begin. But, of course, you don't know what Phase II is yet. Let's get on with that. First, you are to be allowed to see the machine. Not many may do that." And he walked to the golden door and opened it.

The room beyond was no bigger than a closet, and it was lined in black velvet like the inside of a jewel box. On a velvet table in its center stood the Hieronymus Machine. Ellen looked at it and drew in her breath.

Its heart was a single glowing globe the size of a basketball. Smoky as an opal, it flickered and changed color constantly, from pale green to blue to deepest purple and back again. Its hard, perfectly spherical edges seemed to melt and flow beneath the eye. One had the feeling that if one looked at it long enough, one would see everything there was to see.

The globe rested on a small gold pedestal in a field of blackest obsidian, and this field was so heavily contrived as to appear embroidered. Wires and tubes of silver, gold and copper intertwined through it in patterns of terrifying complexity. They were not, one could see, designed to please the eye, but to serve the great central globe. Over the whole device, like a witch's hat, rose a cone of woven black wire.

Ellen stared at it in dread. It was beautiful, but it was also horrible. It seemed to have a life of its own, and it made her think of some monstrous, malevolent spider shining in a dark web.

"Who made that?" she asked in an awed voice.

"We don't know. I don't suppose we ever will. A monk, or several monks—or so they called themselves. We would probably use the word *sorcerers*. They claimed to be followers of the teachings of Hieronymus; perhaps they were. They built this more than a thousand years ago.

"When I found it, it was in a cave, buried in a stone box with a slab of marble on top. How they got that slab on there I don't know. I had to hire a crane to lift it off. Even so, the case had been looted."

"Looted? How could you tell?" But Ellen had guessed the answer already.

"There was a parchment with the machine, rolled up, mildewed, cracked, and covered with Latin writing. I was able to decipher most of it. It said that two crowns had been buried with the machine—one black and one silver. The silver one was missing."

Ellen turned her face away so that he could not see in case she was turning pale. She felt pale. Was this all a trick then? Did he know about her crown? And was it really the same crown? Somehow she felt sure that it was. There was a new sense of danger in the air.

But the King's voice continued calmly enough.

"That was more than a monkey wrench. It was a disas-

ter. For without the silver crown, the whole Hieronymus
Plan was threatened. I didn't know that at the time, of
course—nor even that there was a plan. But it was true
just the same, and I know it now."

Ellen said, trying to keep her voice calm, "How was it
threatened?"

But the King answered rather evasively. "It's nothing
for you to be concerned about. We've located the crown
now, and we know that we will acquire it eventually. We
must acquire it."

Now Ellen began to understand a lot of things, and
again she hoped her face would not betray her. For some
reason, they had to have her crown. That was why Captain Julio had chased her, and that was why Mr. Gates
had given her a ride—he must have known all the time
that she had it in her handbag. And then came the chilling
thought: that was also why her house had been burned
down. She remembered the arson lesson, and she realized
with horror that the King was in charge of that and of
everything else. This kindly, patient, cultured man had
ordered her family burned.

Yet, she realized, she must not permit herself to make
any sign that she knew this. If she did, her chance of res-
cuing Otto and escaping would end instantly. She groped
desperately for something to say. She looked at the machine again.

"Is this . . ." she spoke in a rather gulping voice,
". . . is this machine part of Phase II?"

"It takes your breath away, doesn't it?" The King
glanced sideways at her. "It took mine, too, when I first
saw it." He did not seem suspicious. "No, this is not Phase

II, but you need to see it to understand Phase II. We'll look at that now. Perhaps you've guessed what it is?"

But Ellen had not guessed. The King led the way back into the green room—the Briefing Chamber—touched a spot on the wall, and the elevator appeared. They rode upward.

"We have four more floors above this one," he said, "and they're busy places right now. Top secret, too, I might add."

They got off at the next floor. It was a workshop, and it was busy indeed. Around the wall were workbenches and tables, and at them, hard at work, never speaking, never looking up, were craftsmen—no children these, but gray-haired men with skilled fingers. They were, it seemed, completely hypnotized—"in tune"—for not one of them was aware of the King's presence, or Ellen's.

The King walked to one of the benches and picked up one of several objects that lay on it. He handed it to Ellen.

"There you are," he said. "That's a bit of Phase II."

"But it's a doll!"

"Look at the eyes."

Ellen looked at the eyes, which stared back at her blankly, as dolls' eyes do. They seemed ordinary enough —baby blue, with black, round pupils in the center.

"The pupils," the King explained, "are pure malignite. Just one of these dolls in a little girl's house and she's ours —along with her whole family, and the family next door, too, if they live close enough."

He moved to another bench and handed Ellen a wrist watch. It had black hands and little black dots that marked the minutes.

"Malignite won't make watch-gears," said the King, "but it works beautifully on the face."

On the other benches the craftsmen were making other objects: toy soldiers with black, beady eyes; costume jewelry set with sparkling glass stones of red and blue and green—but always, here and there, a black stone, too.

"Pilot models, of course. We won't attempt mass production. We don't need to, you see. When we give one of our wrist watches to a watch manufacturer and he puts it on, from that minute he'll manufacture watches as we tell him to. Furthermore, he'll pay us for the malignite he puts into them.

"It's a beautifully simple plan, as you can see. In a year or so there will be millions of malignite watches, and dolls, and toys, and other things as well. There's no reason why a little malignite shouldn't be used in every automobile, for instance, and every refrigerator. Will the manufacturers put it in? They will as soon as one of their daughters is given a doll with malignite eyes."

It was, as he said, beautifully simple. Yet it took time for Ellen to grasp it: the size of the plan, the enormity, the dreadfulness of it crept through her mind slowly, the way a sunset slowly darkens the countryside. Malignite everywhere, in every home, in every automobile, like a horrible disease spreading through the world. Then she thought she saw a flaw in the idea.

"But," she said, "all the people who use those things —you can't bring them all here. There isn't room enough."

"No," agreed the King cheerfully. "You're absolutely right. But by then, you see, we won't need to."

He summoned the elevator and they went up one more flight. When they got out, they were again in a workshop like the one below. But with a difference: here there was no variety at all. There were twenty-four craftsmen working with swift and calm efficiency, each under the complete and perfect control of the machine in the throne room below.

And on the work table in front of each man, nearly complete, stood a Hieronymus Machine.

Even the King, who had been here before, seemed awed in this hushed chamber.

"Twenty-four more," he said in a quiet voice, "and in another week, when these are finished, each one of them can start making another twenty-four. And so on. In a few months we'll have one for every city, one for every village."

Now you can see why you are to become part of the plan. Because everyone in the world is to become part of it."

The Big Screen

THE question is," said the King, "how do we make you a part of it?"

They were back in the throne room, and he was standing at the windows again, looking out, hands in pockets.

Ellen said not a word. The sight of all those machines, so evil looking, so nearly complete, had given her, at first, a feeling of terrible hopelessness. She had looked at a disaster about to fall upon the world, and the world knew nothing of it at all. Only she knew—she and the King, and the Hieronymus Machine. Unless you counted the workmen who were making the machines, and you couldn't count the workmen, because they obviously did not know what they were doing.

You could not count the King, either. She had realized that with a terrifying flash of intuition when she saw the new machines being built before her eyes. The King was not building them. He had said as much ". . . *each of them* can start making another twenty-four."

The Hieronymus Machine itself was building them. And that meant that the King was not really the King at all. The machine was in control. The King's every action was under orders; he was in tune like the rest of them— only, when he wore the crown, more so.

Right now he was saying, "You're not like your friend Jenny. When we put her on the screen, she gets in tune, and she does it a little more easily each time. She'll come around. But you . . ." He paused, and then added, as if to himself, "Of course, there's the big screen."

Ellen, grasping for time, to keep him talking while she tried to think, said:

"The big screen? What's that?"

She would have to pretend to cooperate, to be interested in the problem of getting in tune. But she had no intention of doing so if she could help it. She was a monkey wrench, the King had said. Very well, she would be a monkey wrench. Only she—and Otto, if she could rescue him, and maybe Jenny—stood in the way of the Plan. But even a small monkey wrench in the gears can stop a bulldozer. She remembered the despised fable: *A little damage can cause a lot of damage*. They had taught her that lesson—now she would use it against them. But how?

"It's outside," said the King. "We have to keep if there because there's danger of feedback."

"What does feedback mean?" The big screen, Ellen realized, must be the playpen thing she had seen through the gate.

"It means that the emanations from this screen are so

powerful that they might affect the Hieronymus Machine itself—even though it starts them in the first place. You might say it's like shouting so loudly you deafen your own ears.

"That screen would get you in tune all right. But with a mind like yours, we don't like to use it. You are, we think, potentially extremely valuable to us. And that screen has . . . unpleasant side effects."

Ellen noticed, not for the first time, the odd way the King had of switching from "I" to "We" when he spoke. Now she realized that when he said "we", he meant the Hieronymus Machine. So the machine thought she was potentially valuable. *And* a monkey wrench. She wished she knew why.

"You can see for yourself, if you like," said the King. Ellen walked to the window and looked out. There was a man in the playpen thing—the big screen—and he seemed to be trying to get out.

"That man," said the King, "was trained for a mission of vital importance. But when we sent him, he failed completely. He went to pieces. So now he is being re-trained. As you can probably see, he doesn't like it. That's *one* of the side effects."

The man on the screen was running feebly from side to side, as if he wanted to climb the low fence that surrounded it. But each time he reached the fence, something seemed to pluck him back, so that he turned blindly and ran the other way. His face was horribly twisted as if he were in pain, but even so, Ellen recognized him.

"Oh," she cried, "poor Mr. Gates!"

So, at last, she gave herself away.

The King looked at her in puzzlement for a moment. Then he walked across the room and flicked a small switch on the wall. A voice spoke from the ceiling.

"Yes, Your Majesty."

"Bring 719-M to the throne room immediately," said the King, and he clicked the switch off.

A minute later Mr. Gates was escorted—and, in part, supported, for he seemed terribly weak—into the room by two enormous black-clad figures. One of them Ellen recognized: it was the friendly fat man, the one who had given her the sandwiches (it seemed so long ago!) in the little park near the post office. So even he was one of them. The other was a woman, the first woman Ellen had seen in the castle, and she was even bigger and fatter than the man.

Mr. Gates stared at Ellen with a dazed expression. Then his face changed, and he stumbled toward her, pointing.

"She's the one!" he cried in a high, hoarse voice. "She's the one that ran away! That's Ellen Carroll!"

They held him back. The fat man looked at her sharply.

"Yes," he said. "She is the one." Then he smiled at Ellen, friendly as ever. "Don't you remember me?"

"I remember you," Ellen said.

The fat man nodded toward the woman. "You see?" he said. "I told you my wife was fatter than I am."

Now the King spoke to Ellen and his words were made all the more menacing by the sweet, gentle look in his eyes and the patient expression on his face.

"Where is the silver crown?" he asked. And when Ellen did not answer, he added softly, "We will get it, you know. We will get it no matter what we have to do to you."

Otto the Traitor

JENNY said, "You've really got them in a bind."

"I don't see exactly why."

They were talking through the gap, each sitting on her own bed.

"I do. They want to get you in tune. But they want the silver crown even worse."

Ellen had been sent under guard back to her solitary room after she had, for the tenth time, refused to answer the King's question. Plans were now being made for her future, she could be sure of that. Meanwhile she was telling Jenny what had happened. To make sense of it, she had to tell her the whole story.

They had learned by listening carefully that there was a guard on duty now at the end of the hall, but if they talked quietly he could not hear. They did not think he was frantically interested in what they said in any case. He was snoring.

"Maybe so," Ellen said, "but I'm afraid they'll just try to do both."

"But that's it. They can't."

"Why not?"

"If they put you on the big screen and turn up the power, you'll be brainwashed. You won't remember where the crown is. You won't remember anything except what they teach you. That's really what the big screen is for. But, you see, they won't want to do that with you. Not until they get the crown."

"I wonder why they want it so badly? They've got the black one."

"Because the silver one is stronger. As long as they don't have it—or destroy it—it's a threat. They're in danger."

"You mean if I wear the silver crown, and they wear the black one . . ."

"You can beat them. You control the machine."

"Are you sure?"

"Yes. It's one of the things you know when you're in tune. I can't tell why, but I know it."

"Then," Ellen said, "I've got to get the crown and bring it here."

"But they'll take it away from you."

"Not if I can get it to the throne room—to the machine. And put it on."

"No," Jenny agreed. "Then they can't. But how are we going to do that?"

"Will you help?"

"If I can."

"Then listen . . . No. Throw your blanket through

again. I'll climb over."

Ellen had now become adept at sliding through the gap, and a minute later she and Jenny were sitting side by side on the bed, laying out a plot.

Problem number one, they decided, was to get out of the castle, back to the cave, and dig up the crown. They should do this quickly, because they had no doubt that even now hideous schemes were being hatched in the tower. Ellen told Jenny her theory about the stream and the crevasse. With luck, that would be their escape route. But supposing they did get that far: what then?

"Then," Ellen said, "I think we should head over the pass, down to the highway, and find my Aunt Sarah. She'll get a bunch of police, and they'll force a way into the throne room."

"No," Jenny said. "That won't work. Don't you see? As soon as the police get on the black paths, or into the castle, they'll do what the machine tells them. Every now and then somebody does wander in here—a hunter or a hiker—and that's what happens. The King likes it—new recruits."

"Anyway," she added after a moment, "they'd probably catch us before we got through the pass."

"Then," Ellen said desperately, "there's only one thing we *can* do. We've got to get the crown and sneak it into the throne room. But how can we?"

They puzzled over this in silence, and then Ellen said:

"Do you suppose they'll take me up to the throne room again? To talk to the King?"

"I expect they will—to try to get you to tell where the crown is."

"And if I had it with me *then*—in my pocket . . ."

"Oh, Ellen, *yes!* That would work. Then you could just put it on your head and you'd have them."

"Then I've got to get it now, and get back in here, and be here when they come."

"But the guard. Suppose he wakes up?"

And at that precise moment there came a rap at the door. They both realized, to their horror, that the snoring had stopped some time ago. A key turned in the lock. The guard must have heard every word.

But when the door opened it was not the guard at all.

It was Otto, looking proud of himself, calmly twirling the key on a chain around his finger. In the other hand he held a blowgun, loaded with a dart.

"Hello," he said. "How's your ankle?"

"Otto!" cried Ellen, running toward him. Since her intentions were obvious, he ducked behind the chair. Glad as he was to see her, it was clear he was not going to be hugged by a girl.

"Cut that out," he said, but in a pleased voice, "or I'll put you to sleep, too."

"You're Otto?" said Jenny incredulously. "But how . . . ? That's not possible!"

"It is possible. They taught me how to use a blowgun, so I used it. And I stole *all* the darts. Anyway, who are you?"

It took perhaps fifteen minutes of explaining to get things straightened out.

What puzzled Jenny was how Otto, having been in

tune, had nonetheless been able to escape, or had even wanted to escape. Otto himself was none too sure on this point.

"They *thought* I was in tune, and I guess I was, part way at least. But in the blowgun class they turned it off. They almost always do, in the classes." Both girls knew this was true. "And all of a sudden I remembered seeing Ellen, and I decided to find her."

What puzzled Ellen was how he had got by the guard.

"I used the blowgun—a dart with some stuff they call curare on the tip. He won't move for hours. At least, that's what they taught us."

What puzzled Otto, at first, was where the crown was.

"Didn't you bring it?"

"No. I buried it. In the cave."

"Where in the cave?"

"Near the front door."

But he wanted to know *exactly* where, and finally Ellen said in some exasperation:

"I don't know *exactly* where. I mean, I didn't measure it or anything, but I can find it when we get there."

"Well, then," Otto said, "let's go and find it."

"That's what we were talking about when you came in. But we didn't know how to get out past the guard." Quickly she outlined their plan to Otto.

He was immediately enthusiastic. "The guard's out like a light. But he'll wake up in four or five hours, so we'd better go now. It takes that long to get there and back."

"*If* it's the same stream—if it really goes to the cave."

"It must be the same one," he said. "There aren't any

other streams near here." And he knew, for he had hunted through that forest for days.

They passed the guard, lying on his side, rigid, his eyes open but unseeing. Ellen stared at him. He looked dead.

"It's all right," Otto said. "He's not dead. Curare just paralyzes you. He'll be okay when he comes to. Come on. We've got to hurry." And as they tiptoed past him, Ellen could see that the guard was, in fact, breathing.

They walked down the spiral staircase in single file, Ellen leading the way at first. When they got to the iron gate she paused three seconds to listen for voices. She heard nothing, and Otto charged ahead, still holding his blowgun.

"Come on," he said. "We've got to hurry." Ellen wondered at this; it was, after all, *her* plan, her expedition. He was certainly taking charge in a rush. Still she could not be seriously annoyed. She was too glad to have him there. Anyway he was right; they did have to hurry.

They rounded the last circle and reached the bottom in the same absolute blackness Ellen had found before. Now their problem was to stay together, for they could not see one another at all. Ellen felt a hand clutch hers.

"Here," Otto's voice said, "put your hand on my shoulder. Jenny, you put your hand on Ellen's shoulder. Then we'll know where we are." They stepped into the water, felt its flow, and headed upstream in a miniature snake dance.

As it turned out, the thing was absurdly simple. Ellen had feared there might be deep pools they would have to swim in the pitch dark, but the water stayed obligingly ankle-deep, the bottom smooth and hard. They sloshed steadily forward for ten or fifteen minutes, the splash of their feet in the water the only sound. Otto had thrust his blowgun into his belt and held his arms out in front of his face. Occasionally they strayed from midstream, and then his fingers would touch the rock wall, cold and wet, on one side or the other.

At last, just as she had in her dream, Ellen saw a speck of light ahead of her, as uncertain as a firefly.

"I see daylight!"

"I do, too!"

"So do I!"

Two more minutes and they were out of the dark. A streak of blue sky appeared overhead, vague as a crack in a plaster ceiling but growing quickly wider. They could make much better progress now, and Ellen, not having to worry about what the next step would bring, could think.

What she thought was this: they were going ahead with a plan she had conceived before Otto had appeared. Her chief motive for taking the silver crown back to the throne room had been to rescue Otto. But now Otto had rescued himself. Therefore she wondered: Would it not be safer, and in the long run wiser, not to go back? In a day, or two at the most, all three of them could be out of the mountains, back in civilization, back into sanity. Or was this being selfish? What about all the other poor children back there, being trained in evil, being taught to be criminals? And what about Phase II?

She thought about this as she walked. The crevasse had widened now so that most of the time it was not necessary to wade. Their progress was swift and straight. She watched for the cave and kept thinking. She called to Otto.

"Yes?" He did not pause.

"Wait," Ellen said. "We don't need to walk so fast. It makes my side hurt."

"Yes we do. We've got to get the crown."

"I know that. But I'm wondering—do we really have to go back? I mean, now that you're out, shouldn't we just go on through the pass the way we were going in the first place? And take Jenny with us?"

"I guess we could. But let's get the crown first, and then decide."

Otto seemed strangely unconcerned, but to Ellen it seemed a most important point to be decided. For one thing, if they weren't going back it meant they weren't in *quite* such a hurry.

Or were they? When the King learned they were missing from the castle—and he would learn that the instant the guard recovered, and maybe sooner—someone would surely be sent to catch them and bring them back. Probably several people—a whole expeditionary force. They could block the pass. So maybe they were in even more of a hurry. She trotted along, keeping up with Otto. Jenny brought up in the rear.

The crevasse widened and ran as straight as a city street. Far ahead she saw a gray jumble of boulders.

"We're getting there."

"I know. I see them."

"See what?" Jenny had never been there.

"Those rocks up ahead. That's where the cave is."

Ellen felt excited, not only about getting the crown, but about seeing the beautiful cave again. It seemed to her almost like home, or the nearest thing to a home she had.

In another ten minutes they were at the back door. Otto had already disappeared inside. Would the crown be there? Ellen had a quick dread that someone might have been there after her and dug it up. Had she covered the hole carefully enough? Everyone who has ever buried a treasure has had the same thoughts.

Apparently she had, for Otto was up near the front door searching, and could not find it. Ellen and Jenny joined him. Jenny was staring at Otto in a rather odd way.

"Where is it?" His voice was impatient.

Ellen looked. She had, after all, done a good job, considering how stiff her ankle had been and how hungry she had been. At first she could not find the spot herself. Then she remembered: she had marked the wall with an *X*. There it was. She knelt down and dug.

In a moment she was brushing the gravel from the crown. It lay in her hand, beautiful, warm and silvery, its blue stones shining.

Jenny said, "Oh!" in admiration.

But something had happened to Otto. He looked, all at once, strange. Then he began to shout, in a sort of insane excitement:

"We found the crown! We found the crown!"

He shouted this over and over again—five times in all —at the top of his lungs, in a high, trumpeting voice.

Ellen was alarmed. Had he suddenly gone mad? She stared at him, his head thrown back, his eyes strange, his blowgun thrust in his belt . . .

His belt? She had no belt. Nobody in the castle had a belt. But Otto had, of black leather, with a shiny black metal buckle. Then she thought of the doll with the black pupils, and the watch with the black hands. She reached out, grasped the belt, and gave it a fierce pull. It had been hastily made. It snapped and came loose in her hand. She threw it as hard as she could; flying end over end like a shiny black snake it sailed out the door of the cave and plopped into the brook, where it floated away downstream. The blowgun clattered to the ground.

Otto looked bewildered, and tears suddenly streamed into his eyes. But Jenny kept her head.

"Ellen!" she cried, "It's a trick, don't you see?" She snatched the crown from Ellen's hand, and before they could move she was out the front door of the cave and leaping up the boulders like a chamois. She vanished into the forest.

Ellen was stunned. "Jenny stole the crown," she said in dismay. "Otto! We've got to catch her!"

But Otto only said in a sad voice, "She was right. It was a trick." Even as he said it, the black-clad figures filled both doorways, led by the grim face of Captain Julio. They were ambushed.

Then Otto moved. Swiftly, efficiently, with hatred in his eyes, he picked up the blowgun, had a dart in his hand, put it in, leveled the gun. His cheeks made a *"poof"* of air, and one black shape rolled on the rocky floor and did not move.

Another dart, another puff—one more down. He got three in all, but it was hopeless, of course. There were too many. "Rush them," growled Captain Julio. Black arms seized Otto roughly, threw him down, pinned his arms, and the blowgun was theirs.

But Jenny had got away.

Jenny

THE King's mask had changed. Gone was the gentle, tweedy, patient scholar who had talked to Ellen so pleasantly. The new mask was cold anger, and the blue eyes were chips of ice. He sat on the gold-covered throne in a stark black robe, and the black crown lay on the table beside him. The fat man and Brother Michael stood by the throne awaiting orders; Captain Julio, Ellen and Otto waited in silence to hear their fate. The golden door was closed; the Machine Master was hidden.

The machine, Ellen thought, was angry. Or can a machine be angry? At any rate it had decided that the King was to be angry.

"You," he said to Captain Julio in a brittle British voice as hard as a knife edge, "have failed again. You have let the crown slip away. We will deal with you later." And at his instruction, Brother Michael summoned two guards and Captain Julio was led away to the underground dungeon. His sinister face was dark and grim. Ellen did not feel sorry for him.

"You," the King turned to Otto, "betrayed your orders."

"You," the King said to Ellen, "will never see the silver crown again.

"Both of you are to undergo a complete reconditioning at maximum force on the big screen. Unfortunately"— but the cold voice contained no regret—"this will be rather painful, and it will result in a total loss of both memory and personality. You will know and remember only what we teach you. You will be what we create. But since neither of you knows the whereabouts of the silver crown, your memory is no longer of any consequence. We will now get you properly and permanently in tune.

"As for the crown, we will, of course, capture it and the girl." In that, Ellen thought sadly, he was probably right. Before they had begun the slow march back to the castle, Captain Julio had dispatched half his men— twenty in all—to capture Jenny. And she was sure more had been sent since. Evidently they had failed so far. But Jenny was just one frightened girl. Against so many, what chance had she? Where could she go?

And on the march, Otto had tried to explain to Ellen.

"They told me the King was my father," he said miserably. "They told me the crown was his and that someone had stolen it. And when I was in the castle, I believed everything they said. Then they gave me the blowgun and that black belt to wear . . ."

"Poor Otto. You couldn't help it."

"They told me to trick you into telling where it was.

And if you wouldn't tell, to help you escape. And when you found it, to shout for help. But when you pulled the belt off, the whole thing . . . stopped. But then it was too late."

"At least you tried to fight them in the end."

"I got three of them." He brightened a little. "Four, if you count the guard."

As they walked back, surrounded by the enemy, he had stayed close to Ellen's side. When he spoke to her again, it was in a voice as low as a whisper.

"Do you think when we get back to the castle, back on the black paths, that I'll get in tune again?"

"I don't know. Probably. You were before."

"I *hate* it," he said fiercely. "It's like . . . like being somebody else. I'm going to try not to."

The first time Otto had stepped on one of the black paths, late at night, hunting for food, it had caught him unaware. But this time he knew what to expect, and as they approached the gate, he whispered to Ellen again:

"Put your hand on my shoulder."

She did. And when they stepped onto the dark malignite, she felt his hand grasp hers, pull it off his shoulder, and squeeze it in a grip so tight it hurt. His eyes were closed with effort. Hand in hand they walked through the front door of the castle. Finally he let go.

"I did it," he whispered. His forehead was wet.

But what was the use? For now it was all over. There was the king, sitting on the throne before her, pronouncing their doom. She stole a quick look at the door leading out—out to the green room, out to the elevator. But half a dozen of Captain Julio's men stood guard in front of it.

Beyond the King were the bay windows. Supposing she could dash that far before they caught her—could she throw one open and leap out? But it was seven stories down. She would surely break a leg, if not her neck.

As her eyes darted around the room, they fell on Otto. Everyone else was watching the King—everyone but Otto. He was bent over, hidden behind the bulk of the fat man, and staring at the carpet near the golden door.

With his sharp tracker's eyes Otto had seen something no one else had noticed: there were small, muddy footprints, barely visible, leading to the door. His own shoes were still damp from the long walk through the stream. But he had not been near the golden door, nor had Ellen. Still bent, he crept across the room, carefully keeping the fat man (who was facing the other way) between himself and the King.

He saw that the door was not, after all, fully closed. There was a small crack, through which he peered with one eye. He reached inside, then withdrew his hand swiftly.

"Ellen!" he shouted, interrupting the King most audaciously, *"Catch!"*

His hand moved with his deft, knife-throwing motion, and a streak of light shot across the room, striking Ellen on her right wrist. She clutched it.

It was the silver crown. And now its blue stones flashed with a fierce brilliance that dazzled the eyes of everyone in the room.

Ellen stared at it. Then, with a poise and dignity she did not feel, she placed it on her head. Walking in her most queenlike manner, she crossed the room, opened the golden door wide, and put both hands on the great globe.

"From now on," she said. "everyone in this castle will do exactly what I say."

And at her feet, half-hidden under the machine, Jenny rubbed her eyes and sat up.

"There was no air in here," she said. "I guess I fainted dead away."

Good Queen Ellen

Ellen had spoken in the clear voice of confidence, but she was not at all sure that what she said was true. She merely hoped it was, and as she watched the ominous group before her she tried not to tremble. She scarcely dared look at the black-clad guards standing before the throne room door. Within seconds they could charge forward and seize her.

But they did not. Instead, as she watched, a quiet and wonderful change took place. All their attention had been riveted on the King; now, one by one, they turned their eyes to her, and they did not move. More: their expressions changed; the grim hardness on their faces softened and melted away, and a few of them looked as if they might actually smile, if they had not forgotten how. It was as if the emanations coming from the machine, until now so relentless and so harsh, had suddenly turned to something gentler and more cheerful, more human.

Only Otto was not staring at Ellen. He was watching the others, and he, too, saw the change.

"Ellen," he said, almost in a whisper, "you've got them."

"Have I?" she whispered back. "I hope so."

Then, gathering her courage, she made the test. Somehow she knew exactly what she wanted to do first.

"Brother Michael," she said.

"Yes, Your Majesty."

He used the words simply, naturally, inevitably. Yet they sent a surge of joy and relief through Ellen, for they meant that he, at least, now accepted her as the leader. She stole a look at the King. He was sitting bolt upright, motionless, with a dazed expression on his face.

"If I give orders, you and the others will obey them?" She worded it as a statement, but it came out as a question.

"Yes, Your Majesty. We have no choice, as long as you wear the silver crown, and we are in tune."

"Then you will all stay in place, exactly where you are, until I give permission to move."

She knew what she must do, but now she hesitated, for she was afraid at this crucial moment to step away from the machine.

"Otto," she said. "You'll have to help me." She knew Otto was not in tune. But she did not trust any of the others. Not for this.

"Okay," said Otto. "What should I do?"

"Open one of the windows. The one in the middle."

Otto opened it easily.

"Now take the black crown and throw it onto the

screen outside the window." Ellen could not have explained exactly why she wanted this done, beyond the fact
that she wanted to get the crown out of the throne room,
out of the King's reach.

But Otto asked no questions. He took the black crown
to the window—watching the King warily as he went.
Now all eyes in the room were on him. He was carrying
what had been, until moments ago, the weapon of power,
the symbol of authority, for them all. Without hesitation
he tossed it in an accurate arc to the center of the screen,
where it lay like a wreath of ebony—but not for long. In
a moment it turned before their eyes a dull cherry-red,
then crimson, white, and finally a fiery, blinding blue. At
last, with a muffled *boom* like an underground explosion,
it vanished. A cloud of purple smoke hung over the
screen. In a wisp of late afternoon wind, it crawled slowly
away over the castle grounds, over the black paths, and
lost itself in the leaves of the forest.

The little group in the throne room watched the cloud
in fascination until it disappeared. Then the King, with a
long and dreadful sigh, slumped to the floor and lay still.
He had turned deadly pale, and his eyes were closed.

"Otto," said Ellen in alarm. "Look at him. Is he dead?"

Otto leaned over the fallen shape. "No. He's still
breathing."

"Thank goodness," said Ellen.

"Why do you care? He's horrible. Think of all the
things he did."

"No," Ellen said. "He's not horrible. You see, he didn't
really do them. I expect, when he recovers, he'll turn out
to be nice." Her statement puzzled Jenny and Otto, but

she did not pause to explain it. Everyone in the room was looking at her expectantly, and she knew she had to start, finally, being a real queen. She had to give orders.

She called on Brother Michael again. He was, she decided, to be her Prime Minister. He would also serve as her envoy to the outside world. But first there were urgent things to be done in the castle itself.

"Brother Michael, do you know about Phase II?"

"A little, Your Majesty."

"You needn't say 'Your Majesty'," Ellen said, though she rather liked it. "Do you know about the new Hieronymus Machines being built?"

"Up in the tower? Yes, Your M . . . Miss."

"Do you know about the malignite watches and dolls and the other things?"

He did.

"All that is to be stopped at once. And the machines that are nearly finished must be taken apart again."

This was only the beginning of a series of instructions. Ellen gave them crisply and efficiently, as if she had had hours to think about them rather than minutes. The orders were:

As many men as necessary were to carry the King to a room where he could be locked in, for Ellen was not *sure* what he would be like when he woke up. But he was to be made comfortable and looked after as necessary.

All classes were to be suspended. All routines other than classes would continue.

Captain Julio was to be kept locked up and guarded. In tune or not, she did not trust him.

Brother Michael listened carefully, and then excused

himself from the throne room. In a few minutes four young men came in and carried off the still-unconscious King.

Half an hour later, Brother Michael returned to report that all orders had been carried out. The dismantling of the machines would take a few hours, but was already under way.

"Now," said Ellen, "I want to know about the road and the bus. Where does the driveway go that leads from the castle gate?"

"It joins the road that leads over the pass. That road goes down to the highway. It isn't used anymore, except by us." It must be, Ellen realized, the other end of the broken road she and Otto had abandoned.

"As soon as possible," Ellen said, "I want the bus, and two drivers, and you, to go down to the highway, find the police, and tell them . . . just tell them we need help. And then I want you to make a telephone call." And she gave him her Aunt Sarah's name and address.

For Ellen had been thinking hard. And though she did not know what to do with the strange establishment she had won—or rather, she and Otto and Jenny had won—she could see at least one thing with certainty: she was going to need help.

The fat man, whose job in the castle might be called Captain of the Guard, had been standing in silence all this time. Now he spoke:

"There is one other order, Your Majesty, that you have forgotten." And he, at least, remembered how to smile, for he smiled when he said it.

Yet his words sent a feeling of dread through Ellen,

for she half-knew what he was going to say, and she was afraid to think about it. But she said:

"And what is that?"

"There are some prisoners still in the fourth sub-basement dungeon. . ." (The voices she had heard!) ". . . I think perhaps you know who they are, and that you will want them released."

Now Ellen did begin to tremble. It was true; she hoped she knew who they were, and she dared not ask, nor hope too strongly, nor even think very much about it, for fear she might be wrong. Otto stared at her mystified, and so did Jenny and even Brother Michael. The prisoners were, as Jenny had said, secret.

Ellen said only: "Yes. Please do release them."

And she did not stop trembling, nor could she breathe properly, nor think clearly of anything at all until the fat man reappeared. Behind him walked Ellen's mother, her father, and David and Dorah. They looked tired and pale and rather dirty, but they were alive. The tired look gave way to disbelief, then joy, then tears, and then quite a lot of laughter, when they saw Ellen, looking moistly queenlike with her silver crown on her tangled hair—which, as her mother noted very soon, seemed not to have been combed in a month.

Not many hours later, Ellen made a decision that only a queen could make. She made it alone, without advice from anyone. While she wore the crown, and while the machine was present in the castle, she ruled a kingdom—a small one, true, but within it she was an absolute monarch. As she gave orders and saw them obeyed, she grasped what the King had never quite said, and Jenny had only dimly perceived: that whoever wore the black crown was the slave of the machine, but whoever wore the silver crown was its master. She had, finally, subjects and a real castle, although it was a dreary place compared to the gay palace she had once dreamed of. She realized that if she had gone ahead—or let the machine go ahead —and finished building the other machines the King had shown her, she could have eventually ruled a very large kingdom indeed. But that idea was so repulsive, so horrible, that she put it out of her mind.

For the machine was evil. She knew it was evil even though it was now, in a sense, hers. It was evil not necessarily in itself—for how could a machine know "good" from "bad"?—but because it was dangerous, and it was dangerous because it was too powerful, no matter who wore the crown, no matter who controlled it. And besides, she thought, suppose I should lose the crown? And she realized that until she came to the throne room and put on the crown, the machine had been—*must* have been—acting entirely on its own. Unless, perhaps, it was acting on instructions given to it long ago by someone else wearing this same silver crown. In any case, this must never be allowed to happen again.

So she reached her decision: she would abolish her kingdom forever. She would destroy the Hieronymus Machine.

Yet this must be done carefully. She had in her charge a castleful of people who had been completely dominated by the machine, some of them for years. Even now, while she was ruling it, *it* was ruling *them*. She controlled them while the machine existed. But she did not know what they would do when they were suddenly freed. So she decided to wait until the police arrived. Meanwhile, she would get things ready.

How to destroy it? Thoroughly and forever, so that it could never be rebuilt? She remembered what the King had said about "feedback", and she also remembered what had happened to the black crown. She summoned her Captain of the Guard and asked him: could the machine be carried?

The fat man did not know. As long as he could recall, it had always been where it was, in the room with the golden door. But when he tried, he was able to lift one side of it by putting his hands under the obsidian base. It was heavy, however. Four more guards were called. One to a corner, with the fat man directing, they wrestled it into the elevator, down, and out of the castle through the main door. They set it down beside the big screen and waited. Ellen stayed with them, and in a little while Otto and Jenny joined her.

Thus it was that when the caravan arrived—led by Brother Michael in the bus, then two police cars, then a jeep containing a huge dog, a man dressed all in brown, and a beautiful golden-haired lady—they were greeted by a strange sight. In front of the castle three children, one a small girl wearing a silver crown, were directing five black-clad men as they lifted a strange, glittering globe and placed it in the middle of a black screen. As they watched, the globe, which seemed to be surrounded by wires, flashed angrily in red and blinding violet and then, with a clap like thunder, vanished in a giant sphere of smoke.

The police, thinking they had seen some kind of a bomb, leaped from their cars and ran forward, drawing their pistols as they came. There were six of them. They stopped when they reached the children.

"You won't need the guns," said the girl with the crown rather haughtily. "I have everything under control."

Then, before the long explanations began, a beautiful and miraculous thing happened: birds came. As the smoke cleared away, they flew in by hundreds, by thousands, from the forest in every direction. They filled the sky over the castle, soaring, twittering, diving, cheeping, cawing, a ballet and a chorus of joy at having got rid of the evil emanations. Among them flew a great flock of crows, and after a few low swoops of inspection one of these detached itself from the rest and settled on Otto's shoulder.

"Richard eat," it said.

Safe at Oakstable

AT THE Blue Hill, Ellen had got up first and sat alone on the wide, sunny patio between Aunt Sarah's house and the garden. She had the silver crown in her lap, and she played with it absentmindedly as she watched two woodpeckers chase two jays out of their tree and back to the woods where they belonged. The blue stones in the crown twinkled gently, as they had when she first found it lying on her pillow. It had been some force from the machine, she supposed, that had made them glow so brightly. The crown was now only a beautiful toy, of uncertain value but hers forever.

The police had at least believed Ellen's claim that it was her own (though not until this had been verified by Aunt Sarah, and the postcard produced, duly cancelled and dated). But that was just about all they would believe. They listened politely while Ellen, Otto and Jenny told of their struggle against the black crown and the

Hieronymus Machine.

"Where is this machine?"

"Well, it exploded."

"And the crown?"

"It exploded, too."

"I see."

And the policemen exchanged knowing smiles. But they did seem to accept the word of all concerned that the King had been the leader of this strange and obviously illegal establishment. It was, they decided, some kind of a huge school, run by a rich madman, very likely a religious crank. What they thought of the classrooms, the distorted textbooks and the workshops, Ellen never knew.

They turned the kidnapped children over to the State Juvenile Administration; the grownups were sent to a State institution for psychiatric examination. The worst damage any of them seemed to have suffered was a complete loss of memory of the whole period they had been dominated by the machine.

The King they took to a hospital where he was examined by numerous internists, neurologists, psychiatrists, psychologists and cardiologists, and was pronounced to be in a deep coma. So far as Ellen knew he had not yet waked up.

The speed with which Brother Michael had found not only the police and Aunt Sarah but Mr. Carver, too, was easily explained. For Aunt Sarah, as Ellen had speculated she would, had already begun a search; she and the police had tracked the children as far as Mr. Carver's house. When he learned that they had not made it over the pass he, too, joined the hunt.

So now they had all come to the Blue Hill: Ellen, Otto, Jenny, David, Dorah, Aunt Sarah, and Mr. Carver. As Ellen had told Otto, the house had about thirty rooms, so there was plenty of space for them all. Only Ellen's parents were not there; they had gone back to the city to find a new house to live in. Richard had come, however, and so had the dog King, and the two had quickly struck up an unbreakable friendship.

Ellen, at this moment, felt no friendship at all toward people who slept late. Why should a queen, who has conquered a fearsome enemy, have to go hungry just because she wakes up early?

Just then Otto appeared, looking back over his shoulder. He came through a door that led from the kitchen. He had a furtive look on his face and a jelly doughnut in each hand. When he saw Ellen, he started, then sat down and handed her a doughnut. He removed two more from his pockets.

They sat and ate in silence until the first two doughnuts were gone. This morning was, in a sense, the first chance they had had to sit and think. They had arrived at the Blue Hill late the night before, and before that they had been too busy doing things, telling things, and hearing things.

Ellen, for example, had been no more eager to tell her story than to hear her family's, which was shorter and simpler: They had, before the fire, received a phone call. An unknown voice told them that Ellen had been kidnapped; that if they wanted to see her alive again they must go at once to an address the voice gave them. Then the phone clicked off. They went, of course, only to be kidnapped themselves at gunpoint and locked up in the dungeon as hostages, in case they were needed to force Ellen to bring the crown to the castle.

Now, sitting and eating doughnuts, Ellen and Otto began the long game—it would go on for weeks, possibly for the rest of their lives—which might be called, "What I Don't Understand Is . . ."

"What I don't understand," Otto said, "is why you decided the King wasn't so bad after all."

"I only *thought* so at first; I wasn't really sure of it. But when I was standing close to the machine, I saw a sign on it—two signs—that you couldn't see."

"What kind of signs?" Otto started the second doughnut.

"Two little brass plates. One was in some language—Latin, I think. The other was in English. Old-fashioned English, like King Arthur. It said:

> *Who weareth the black crown, I rule.*
> *Who weareth the silver crown, ruleth me.*

I think the Latin one said the same thing, and the English was just a translation. But anyway, do you see what that meant?"

"Nope," said Otto, reaching the jelly part.

"It meant that the King wasn't using the machine at all. The machine was using him."

"The machine could think? All by itself?"

"It must have."

"And that's why you wrecked it." His face grew bright with understanding. "And *that's* why the King fainted!"

"Yes. I wrecked it because it was too dangerous."

"It was sort of dopey, if you ask me. All those fables and things."

"No," Ellen said. "It wasn't. It had to . . . sort of feel its way. It was testing people. And it was getting smarter all the time."

"What I don't understand," Otto said again, "is how you got the crown in the first place."

"I don't either. Not at all. I'm going to ask Mr. Carver and Aunt Sarah when they come down. They might have figured it out."

"I wish they'd hurry up. I finished two doughnuts and my belly's still empty."

"Don't say belly. It's vulgar."

Later, after breakfast, they did ask Mr. Carver and Aunt Sarah, who were sitting together on a garden bench.

Mr. Carver lit his pipe. "I've thought quite a lot about it," he said. "Some parts we have to guess at. But others seem reasonably sure.

"For one thing, we know that the machine itself was running the show—not the man who called himself the King. We don't even know who he is, and until he comes back to his senses we can't ask. Personally, I doubt that he'll remember. He was too completely hypnotized for too long.

"So we have a machine—built, we are told, by a monk or a sorcerer a thousand years ago. It was built in Spain, I believe, though the King seems to be English. It was called the Hieronymus Machine, and there are many stories about it in medieval literature, particularly in books about the strange religious beliefs that grew up in the Dark Ages.

"Mrs. Fitzpatrick had read about it. And so, once or twice, have I. But I think the King knew a great deal more. I would guess that he was a scholar—perhaps an historian or an archeologist; in any case, somehow he got on the track of the machine, and he found it, still intact. With it he found the black crown. When he touched it (perhaps he even tried it on) he was instantly enslaved.

"The silver crown was missing. It must have belonged to the man who built the machine, and for some reason when he buried it and the black crown, he did not put the silver one with them—though, according to the ancient manuscript the King found, he had intended to.

"Obviously, something went wrong. If you study history, you can guess what happened. Europe a thousand years ago was in chaos, overrun by barbarians from the east, by Moors and Moslem hordes from the south. I think that very soon after Hieronymus, as he called himself, built this machine, his world collapsed around him. In fear, he hid his marvellous invention in a safe place; but before he could hide the silver crown, it was taken from him. Most likely the invaders, whoever they were, killed him and took the crown for its silver and its gems, not realizing what they had.

"By what magic Hieronymus designed the machine, we will never know. The magic is lost, and the machine destroyed. But it was a machine that could, at least in a limited way, *think*. It was meant to be used and controlled through the silver crown. And through the machine in turn, the wearer of the silver crown controlled the one who wore the black crown.

"But when the King found it, the silver crown was gone, and the machine discovered that it could work alone. Or can a machine 'discover'? Anyway, it went on doing what it had been taught to do: that is, to use its power to expand its power; to find more malignite and control more people—and eventually to build more machines like itself. All that must have been planned in the mind of the man who built it a thousand years ago.

"Through the King, the machine got itself transported to a place where malignite was plentiful. It acquired more servants; it built itself a castle; it began testing its powers —flexing its muscles, you might say. That was Phase I. The rest we know. Except . . ."

"Except about Ellen," Otto said.

"Yes," said Mr. Carver. "Except about Ellen. The machine, when it got enough power—enough people— began a search for the silver crown. Perhaps it could sense, somehow, that the crown still existed, though not where it was. But what did it want with Ellen? Why Ellen *and* the crown?

"I have a theory, and it is this: Only a rare kind of person, with an unusual kind of mind, could use the silver crown. We know that Ellen's mind is unusual. For one thing, she was not affected by the malignite—she did not get 'in tune', even on the screen. The King himself told her that she was the only one who didn't. Perhaps Ellen was also the only person who could wear the white crown effectively, who could make it work. Or possibly there were a few others, but she was the nearest, the easiest to capture.

"Very well, you may say—but why not simply kidnap

Ellen and secure the crown, and bring them to the castle separately? The only reason I can think of is this: until Ellen actually put the crown on her head, the machine could not be sure she was the right one. Perhaps, like the glass slipper, it had been tried on others and had not worked. If this was true, then it must also be true that the machine could sense from many miles away that she *was* the right one—but not until she tried it on.

"This whole business of distance is a puzzling one. Obviously the machine could not tell—even up close— where the silver crown was. Otherwise it would have sent Captain Julio to the cave immediately. Yet there was some kind of interaction between them: for example, Ellen and Otto both noticed that as the crown got closer to the machine, its jewels glowed more brightly. Perhaps the crown even had, in some misty way, an energy of its own. It *seems* as if Ellen found her way to the castle entirely by accident. But was it really accidental? Or was the crown somehow guiding her to it? All we can be sure of is what we can see: that when the machine ceased to exist, the jewels stopped glowing.

"Another thing we can puzzle over: Did the machine intend to destroy Ellen and the crown? Had it learned to enjoy wielding its own power—so that it regarded the crown as a threat? Or did it, on the contrary, in its own strange way of thinking, realize that it *needed* the silver crown? Did it feel a want of guidance? Could it foresee a day when it would, you might say, run out of instructions? I think it could only do what it had been taught: build more machines, control more people. Eventually, perhaps, control the world. But what then? If it did not know, it would need the crown, and it would need Ellen.

"So it was quite willing to be as brutal as necessary toward Ellen's family, and to burn down her house—and, indeed, to kill innocent people like Officer Drogue and the store manager, to get her. But Ellen herself was to be treated gently. No force was to be used on her. After all, to the machine, the silver crown and the one who wore it were still its superiors—its creators! If possible, she was to come of her own free will.

"Through its spy system, that is, people it had trained and sent out, or through some other system we know nothing about, the machine found out about Ellen, and located the silver crown. It was thorough. It not only knew about her, but about her family as well, and even about her Aunt Sarah.

"Getting the crown to Ellen was simple enough. She found it on her pillow: I expect there were some expert housebreakers among the graduates of the black castle. They were especially clever to deliver it on her birthday, so she would think it was simply a present.

"Now: enter Arthur Gates, and the fat man, and quite a crew of helpers. They knew their business. Watch and wait until Ellen leaves the house, alone, with the crown. More important—wait until she puts it on her head. She obliged them by doing both immediately; if not, they'd have stood by until she did, or figured out something else. Then, call her family: she's kidnapped. Get the family out—burn the house—the arson squad. Sometime about then the crew must have got word from headquarters, from the machine: She's the one. Bring her in. Bring the crown with her. That made sense, of course, since she had it in her handbag.

"They watched her every step of the way. They could not very well get her away from the police without her knowing it, but they could, and did, get the police away from her by a brutal and effective trick: a senseless murder. It was simple enough after that to trick her into Mr. Gates's car—a new car bought or stolen just for that ride.

"But Mr. Gates, so long dominated by the machine, was not thinking very clearly on his own, nor driving very well. He blundered, gave away the show, and let Ellen escape. They sent their best—or worst—man to recapture her. He, too, failed.

"Then, as we know, in the end she walked into their hands. But coming as she did, in a group of other children and *without the crown,* they didn't know who she was.

"Finally the machine found out who she was, however, and then it seems to have made up its mind to destroy Ellen and the crown. I say 'It seems' because we can't be sure of that even now. It told the King to *act* that way—but it may have been bluff. Since it could not control Ellen's mind, nor, in the end, Otto's either, it may still have thought they knew where the crown was. It could have been trying to frighten them into telling.

"But I believe it had really decided to destroy them, after all its trouble in getting them there. Because I think it had not understood, until she got there, that for the first time in a thousand years it was dealing with someone it *could not control at all.*

"Anyway, it was too late. Because Jenny, as Ellen had realized, knew the ropes. She had been to that tower a hundred times and knew her way around it. So instead of trying to run away, she ran directly to the last place they would look for her—to the machine itself, carrying the crown with her. When she got to the throne room she found it empty, so she hid in the machine's own chamber. She knew they would all be there soon—and then, at last, Ellen could take charge."

Mr. Carver paused and struck a match for his pipe. "And that," he said, puffing between words, "is as close as I can come to telling you what really happened. If anyone has a different theory, he may very likely be right."

Ellen said: "Now that the machine is gone, my silver crown is just a crown. Do you think that if I went back to the cave and put it on, I'd still hear that . . . music?"

"Someday," said Aunt Sarah, "let's go and find out. I'd like to see that cave and the crevasse for myself. Jason —Mr. Carver—can come, too, and Otto can be the guide if Mrs. Fitzpatrick will let him stay with us for a while. I'll write to her and ask if he may." (Ellen had told Aunt Sarah about Otto and the trucks.)

"I'd like to go," Otto said. "As long as there isn't anybody chasing us."

But Ellen had a strange feeling that when they got there, the crevasse and the cave and the hollow tree and all the rest would be gone. Already the whole thing was beginning to feel like something that had never happened.

She felt this, but she did not say it. Otto was looking at Mr. Carver and Aunt Sarah in a peculiar way, and she recalled a conversation he had had with her long ago, as they first approached the crevasse. The two grownups had, after all, been acquainted for days, and here they were sitting together—and rather close, too—on the garden bench. Otto watched them with a mysteriously pleased expression on his face, and then said, addressing them both:

"By the way, how do you like each other?"

Ellen was not sure whether to laugh or be embarrassed. Aunt Sarah may possibly have realized what he meant, for she turned pink.

Ellen said: "Otto, shut up."

"Don't say 'shut up'," Otto said. "It's vulgar."

A Different Conclusion

The following ending was written by Robert C. O'Brien for the British edition of *The Silver Crown*. Though this final chapter is considerably shorter than that of the American edition, it concludes the book in an equally satisfying—and fascinating—way. Best of all, perhaps, is the choice it gives the reader as to which works best, and why.

At Aunt Sarah's house at the Blue Hill, Ellen got up first and sat alone on the wide, sunny patio between the house and the garden. She had the silver crown in her lap, and she played with it absentmindedly as she watched two woodpeckers chase two jays out of their tree and back to the woods where they belonged. The blue stones in the crown twinkled gently, as they had when she first found it lying on her pillow. It had been some force from the machine, she supposed, that had made them glow so brightly. The crown was now only a beautiful toy, of uncertain value.

Nor did Ellen, at the moment, feel particularly queenlike. She wanted breakfast. Why should she, who had conquered a fearsome enemy, have to go hungry just because she had woken up early?

Just then Otto appeared, looking back over his shoulder. He came through a door that led from the kitchen. He had a furtive look on his face and a jelly doughnut in each hand. When he saw Ellen, he started, then sat down and handed her a doughnut. He removed two more from his pockets.

They sat and ate in silence until the first two doughnuts were gone. Then they began the long game—it would go on for weeks, possibly for the rest of their lives—which might be called, "What I Don't Understand Is…"

"What I don't understand," Otto said, "is why you decided the King wasn't so bad after all."

"I only *thought* so at first; I wasn't really sure of it. But when I was standing close to the machine, I saw a sign on it— two signs—that you couldn't see."

"What kind of signs?" Otto started the second doughnut.

Two little brass plates. One was in some language—Latin, I think. The other was in English. Old-fashioned English, like King Arthur. It said:

> *Who weareth the black crown, I rule.*
> *Who weareth the silver crown, ruleth me.*

I think the Latin one said the same thing, and the English was just a translation. But anyway, do you see what that meant?"

"Nope," said Otto, reaching the jelly part.

"It meant that the King wasn't using the machine at all. The machine was using him."

"And that's why you wrecked it." His face grew bright with understanding. "And *that's* why the King fainted!"

"Yes, I wrecked it because it was too dangerous."

"What I don't understand," Otto said again, "is how you got the crown in the first place."

"I don't either. Not at all. Let's ask Aunt Sarah when she comes down. She might have figured it out."

"I wish she'd hurry up. I finished two doughnuts and my belly's still empty."

"Don't say belly. It's vulgar."

Later, after breakfast, when they were all—Ellen, Jenny, Otto (with Richard) and Aunt Sarah—sitting in the garden, they did ask her.

Aunt Sarah answered slowly. "After all the trouble it caused, I am sorry to say *I* sent you the crown. Do you remember when I was in Spain this spring? I found it then in a little curio shop in Barcelona. It was a strange shop selling all kinds of things—horns from famous bulls, Roman artifacts, cheap statues of the Virgin Mary—that sort of thing. I saw the crown and noticed the strange material and workmanship. The proprietor thought it must have been a theatrical prop. Anyway, I bought it and sent it to your mother to give you on your birthday. How those dreadful people found out about it I have no idea."

She was silent a moment; then she took Ellen's hand. "At least," she said, "it proved you really are a Queen."

This was too much for Otto. "A Queen!" he said and leapt to his feet. Then bowing low, "Could I, your Majesty, have another jelly doughnut?"

   "Shut up, Otto," Ellen said.

   "Don't say 'Shut up,'" Otto said. "It's vulgar."